CALLBACKS

Meg Whiteford

First published 2018 by &NOW Books, an
imprint of Lake Forest College Press.

Carnegie Hall
Lake Forest College
555 N. Sheridan Road
Lake Forest, IL 60045

lakeforest.edu/andnow

Lake Forest College Press publishes in the broad spaces of
Chicago studies. Our imprint, &NOW Books, publishes
innovative and conceptual literature and serves as the publishing
arm of the &NOW writers' conference and organization.

ISBN: 978-1-941423-01-1

Library of Congress:

Cover Design by Morgen Malte
Book Design by Jaime Dear
Graphic Design Direction by Emma O'Hagan

Printed in the United States

The writing of this book would not have been possible without the support of Lake Forest College, Madeleine P. Plonsker, Brian Evenson, and the Glen Rowan House staff; the hawk eyes of Dawn Finley and Merkel; and crisis control from Julia Masnik, Emily Milder, Tyler Crumrine, and Barbara. I dedicate these pages to the ensemble.

FOREWORD

About a year and a half ago, I chose Meg Whiteford's *Callbacks* for the Madeleine P. Plonsker Emerging Writers Residency Prize, based on the first fifty pages of the manuscript-in-progress. It was a funny and beautifully written excerpt about a set of contortionist triplets who seemed to be on the shaky rise toward some sort of regional stardom. The strength of the prose was such that it seemed almost impossible to me that this could be someone's first novel.

Now that I've read the novel as a whole, I'm pleased to say that it more than fulfills the promise of that early excerpt. *Callbacks* is one of those rare first novels in which a writer seems to be up and sprinting right out of the gate. It doesn't hurt that Whiteford is a playwright (one of her plays, *The Shape We Make with Our Bodies* was published by Plays Inverse in 2015, and several have been performed in LA and elsewhere), and that this book is in many senses about performance and performing. Whiteford has an intuitive grasp of dialogue and voice. Indeed, for me one of the great strengths of *Callbacks* is the strength of the routines that it offers, the snappiness of the dialogue. I could almost hear these routines in my head as I read them, and found myself imagining the intonation and stances of the characters with a vividness that I rarely encounter when I read fiction. *Callbacks* provides both the satisfaction you get when reading a strong novel and that you come away with after seeing an original and slightly surreal piece of immersive theater.

For me, one of the strengths of the innovative contemporary novel is its ability to cross-pollinate, to blend in other genres and use them to revitalize the long prose form. *Callbacks* has a tempered attention to sound and language that reminds me of poetry. It also offers, almost as perforations in the stripped-down plot, acts, songs and performances, and these drive the book forward as much as the action does. Vaudeville is not only the subject but something that shapes the book as a whole—as do, at various keys points, puppet shows and television. These latter are exceptionally interesting and weird: it's like watching Shari Lewis's Lamb Chop being rewritten by David Lynch. Performance here becomes a means of vacillating between the realistic and the surrealistic, of dislocating the reality of the piece in ways that are sometimes safe and cleanly delineated and sometimes—particularly as the book moves forward—anything but safe. I'd say that *Callbacks* is a realistic book with a surreal core, except that what's the pith and what's the pit keep inverting.

At the heart of the story are the three Starling triplets: Minnie, Esther, and Pearl, with Pearl being the one to narrate the story to us. In their teenhood, they are abandoned by the people who should care for them and end up striking out on their own. They enter a dying vaudeville show run by Bette Bunting in the small town of Sky-on-the-Lake. There, they join with the Bette Bunting Cardinal Five Revue, some of whom accept them, others of whom bridle against them. Five and three become eight while at the same time remaining a separate five and a separate three, with a myriad of combinations within that, some of which threaten to destroy the community as a whole. Whiteford understands the vectors, connections and lines of flight that can criss-cross through such a grouping of women, and understands too where tensions will rise, where cracks will begin to show, both internally and externally. As Pearl tells us, fame and fortune seem to beckon, but things do not go exactly as expected...

If I say much more, I'll give too much away. Better by far, to let Whiteford speak for herself. Enjoy.

—Brian Evenson

❈

Hello! Welcome to Bette's Great 8 Tom Tom Revue! Yes, welcome ladies and gentlemen to the only, that's right, the only all-female variety show on the West Coast. As far as I know, at least.

Our show abounds with delicate roses with abundant talents. We have June the soubrette cross dresser to rile you up with her soothing coos, Charlene the balletic snake charmer with the slithering grace of a female Nijinsky, Kiki our melancholic clown and polymath musician, Blanca the Flaming Beauty with a tongue of steel, Franny the silent siren, and our latest editions, the triple threat triplets, The Starling Sisters, contortionists with voices like canaries to carry your imaginations to faraway lands. They're sure to wind their ways into your hearts, but not before a loop-de-loop around your legs, a pirouette over your shoulders, and a little tap dance on your forehead.

And as always, we'll wrap up the show with a grand finale starring all eight of our charming beauties for your viewing and listening pleasure.

Drinks are two-for-one until six pm and may I recommend the Flaming Blue Tiger. To your left is the loo, in case those drinks get to you. Feel free to cheer the ladies on, but remember, only looking, no touching. We're keeping it clean and we're keeping it friendly.

Sit back and enjoy. Here we go, on with the show!

LITTLE BAD

Mama and Pop made us on their first night together. Pop wooed our mother by picking a rose from the high school trim garden and leaning it around her shoulder. They both grabbed that thorny twig and used it as leverage as they fell in love. Pop rolled cigarettes back and forth against his tongue, as though he were plucking the paper of feathers, preparing a chicken dinner. Our mother, Georgia, nicknamed the Cuckoo, was a songstress, a lounge act at the bar in town—the Little Bad. She was cold in life, hard and judgmental. But on stage she lit up in warm exuberance, all unctuous fabrics thrown over shoulders and tears summoned for dramatic effect. She was but a chickadee herself when she started singing, skipping school to spend her nights at the bar belting notes.

The Little Bad was a lounge on an otherwise abandoned street in a dicey part of our town. The place stood out like a velvety bruised thumb. What with its showy facade and baroque awning, nestled between the clapboard ranch homes with dusty yards, the Little Bad was the peacock among hens who'd seen better days. Mama started out as a cocktail waitress selling watered-down booze and cigarettes to men and sometimes to the men's wives. You might think her would-be husband, our father, was one of these men, a rich man from out of town here to sweep her under his wing to a fairy-tale ending. The boy gets the girl and the girl gets the dresses and gets to live high up in the castle. But no, her would-be husband was The Little Bad's dishwasher.

Pop had a reputation as a fighting man with a temper. He was much older than Mama, with no point of origin. He was much smaller, too. Whereas the Cuckoo spread out with brazen hips and contours, he was compact and efficient in size. His family either came from French Canada, or Scotland, sometimes it was France. Or, he was just a boy from one town over from ours, little Sandpiper Springs. He was known about town for two things: his undefeated county-wide wrestling title in the lowest weight bracket, and his big nose: a behemoth of cartilage that stuck both out and across his otherwise sunken face. "It's a wonder that nose don't topple his beanpole body," folks would say.

"That nose is a sign of bad luck," our mother's superstitious aunts would say—there were six in all.

"That man is going to smell something intoxicating and follow the scent, leaving you behind."

The Cuckoo took to hoarding a lifetime supply of paper perfume samples pulled from magazines, rubbing their conflicting scents on her wrists, neck, and ankles, to keep her suitor around. She played it cool but her aroma suggested otherwise.

At the Little Bad, she sang each night for three hours, sometimes four. The Cuckoo had a habit of singing mainly in whistles, blowing the words through her two front teeth to produce a timbre that toed a thick line between intriguing and repellent. The men at the bar gambled as she sang and didn't pay any attention at all. Sometimes, however, some of them paid too much attention. The Cuckoo would tell her would-be husband the tale of her spurned suitors like it was a badge of desirability. He fought with anyone who looked at the Cuckoo. He'd practice his grappling holds and takedowns, and rope-a-doped his way into Mama's heart. He was violent and loud, and, at first, she resisted his current. One day he threw a bottle of gin at a man who then scratched him from lip to ear with a fishing lure. He removed the lure, cast it to the Cuckoo, and played possum until she took the bait. Sometimes, the only way to triumph against such a shrewd opponent is to question your relationship to the dance. Give in to it, bend, and dodge alongside it.

They married quickly and unceremoniously. The reception was at the Little Bad. The guests (most of whom were the evening's patrons) ate day-old biscuits with clotted cream and drank a bottle of rum apiece. For her wedding present, Pop bought Mama a trailer and parked it on the other side of the town near the river. He wanted to get her away from the Little Bad, give her a better life, but this wasn't the castle she was told she'd get upon betrothal.

Why did this man love her? She was indifferent to him, which was the worst kind of cruelty. Mama Cuckoo sold her soul willingly to the Little Bad and the Little Bad was where her soul would stay for eternity. She had to go there to keep herself alive. It was the glaring difference from the rest of her life, I think, that she craved, a reprieve that sustained her.

She gave birth to us—me (Pearl), Minny, and Esther— five days apart from each other: five, ten, fifteen days of labor. We were identical, yet not twinned, tripled humans with an unaccounted-for five days between the womb and birth.

"What were you doing in there for five days?" Mama Cuckoo asked us later, with eyes thinned to razors, skeptical of our motives.

In a hurry to accommodate their growing family, the Cuckoo and our father hodge-podged our home together. They collected salvaged bits and pieces from dumps scattered around neighboring towns. The trailer itself our father found intact in nearby Stagflower Lake. It was a space no larger than a plastic vending machine egg. They parked it by a lake among many other trailers in a town with little else besides a gas station and a coffee klatch. They stitched together an awning from used t-shirts, made a patio from discarded shoe soles, and decorated a common area with inspirational posters, mismatched bone china and plastic dish sets, an army cot for sleeping quarters, and the collection of amber-colored glass vessels. The tiles of the kitchen were brown laminate imitation brick. The walls were wallpapered cream with a small yellow print of Moonbeam coreopsis. A rotary phone, also yellow, was attached to the wall. Its impossibly long curlicue tail, "makes it easier to reach all my utensils and clip your ears if you backtalk while I'm on the phone," the Cuckoo would say.

"I do have an eye for design!" Our proud father said, as he hung a wooden pineapple above our kitchen sink, stepping back to admire his work. It was in these close quarters where we learned to mimic our mother and contort ourselves to fit into small spaces. I bent around my sister who bent around my other sister who bent around me. Our lives made sense this way. We were all blue-faced babies, newborn walnuts, with bodies no wider than strands of straw.

❁

The roads in Sandpiper Springs were long and interspersed with buildings that all looked the same: cream-colored stucco with rounded corners built low to the ground. Here were consignment shops, a post office; there a Tex-Mex joint, and a gas station promoting two-for-one fountain drinks to go. The space between each business was too far for any sane person to walk down the highway, so you had to drive from place to place—stopping and starting your car, pulling in and out of parking lots. That's the way it went in Sandpiper Springs, you had to shuffle if you wanted to get anything done.

Pop would leave often and when he came home he arrived with presents for us three. Once a tiny baking set, once a plastic pony with rainbow hair, sometimes insects, lizards, and frogs. He read us books in comical voices, bringing the theater of the pages alive. My mother sat motionless from some hidden perch, listening in, her shoulders hunched to disguise her fading beauty, as she waited for him to leave once more and this time take her with him. Whatever anyone might say about her, she was a patient feeder.

Our father took us to the historical museum to kill some time on the odd Saturdays he was home. The museum was another one of those stucco houses but this one was filled with geodes and taxidermied roadkill. Placards lined the hallway explaining the provenance and significance of each relic or fossil. JACKRABBITS, read one, *Jackrabbits are known for their cunning and quick-witted nature.* Next to it was an imprint of a seashell: *Did You Know: Sand is actually made up of eroded shells of creatures who once swam in nearby, but long-gone, saltwater?* We saw our first movie in that museum—a fifteen-minute documentary on the rock toad, narrated by our then-mayor.

"Pick out something useless for yourselves," our father said. Minny chose a wooden pinwheel, Esther a stuffed baby black bear, and I chose an intact geode. My rock came with an instructional slip: *Use a hammer to knock with directed precision to reveal deep-hued quartz. Each geode is completely unique. Some contain quartz, while others are shallow rocks. There is no guarantee your choice contains these crystals, so choose wisely and knock at your own risk.*

Afterwards, we would share a banana split at the dairy bar—I took the chocolate scoop, Esther the strawberry, and Minny the vanilla.

"You three are my scoops of sweetness," Pop said. "I'm one half of the banana and your mother is the other, but where's the a-peel anymore?" He'd order a pie and flirt with the waitress who, almost always, took the bait and sent seconds on the house.

"Ma'am, my ma used to make the best lemon chiffon in all of the state, in my humble opinion. She'd let it rest on the stove until it got those little sugar dew drops on the meringue. Mmm mmmm *mmm!* I can taste it now in this pie, right here. Just as sweet as you are, darling."

Our town was the type of town where necks

were craned at any deviation in step, sound, sight, or rhythm of the day. It was a town of buttoned-up and paranoid cliques of women observing the outside world through slatted blinds, whispering about the bomb, or the unstable border, or other foreign threats when crossing paths in predictable places like the supermarket. They were left alone by men whose jobs took them on the road for days on end.

In a town like this, our family presented quite the scandal. Our mother worked at a bar (a place where men went without their wives), went out, got drunk, and didn't whisper a word when that word could be shouted or sung. Everyone knew our business because we flaunted it without shame. And our father, though he was inclined to short stints away from the coop, was an attentive caregiver when he was around. When he took the time for it, Pop was a gifted storyteller. My favorite of his yarns was a story that he called the People Born Before the Moon. These little people, these little creatures, appeared in a whale's corpse at the bottom of the ocean. They were born there and they died there. They had the same lifespan as the skeleton—which, according to Pop, was about seventy years or so before complete decomposition. But during that small amount of time they invent a whole civilization for themselves.

"It's time compressed," Pop said, though I hadn't a clue what he meant by that.

The People Born Before the Moon were revealed in the tendons of the whale after some ocean scavengers had their way with its body. The People Born Before the Moon were born without eyes or mouths. But these little wormy things called the Bone Devourers, the same creatures that picked away the whale's flesh, ate little holes in the people's faces where two eyes and a mouth should be. The People Born Before the Moon were red, and wore all red clothing and, once their mouths were carved, they drank red drinks and ate red food and even spoke a red language.

"By year five, the little people had invented iron and steel and were building whole towns. And rail lines! They all had the same jobs—moving these calcified bits of marrow they extracted from the whale's bones, also red, everything is red, from the tail of the body to the mouth. There was no government, no hierarchy, they all just worked in harmony."

"Girls, after I die, if anyone finds that story I'd ask that they publish it for me. 'Ship Captain and posthumous author.' I'd like that on my grave." At night he'd construct ships in a bottle made from toothpicks and beer bottles. When he took off on his trips he'd tell us he was setting his ships to sea.

When we were eleven, the Cuckoo painted our trailer a hideous burnt orange. She outfitted the north side with a bit of corrugated metal to serve as an awning.

"It's like our little desert cabana," she said, sitting out there in her folding chaise lounge beach chair at sunset, sipping lemonades and iced tea, fanning herself with trade paperbacks she stole from the Sandpiper Springs Public Library.

"You know girls, in ancient Greece, the master of the house would demand that his servants feed him grapes and fan him with palm leaves," the Cuckoo said.

We enjoyed her game of slave labor. This was our chance to try and please our unsatisfiable mother. We took off to the expanse of our desert backyard hooting and hollering to find palm fronds for fans. Because we had no grapes, we fed her nonpareils instead. The little white beaded chocolate candies were her favorite sweet. While she refreshed herself in the shade, Pop taught us Greco-Roman wrestling moves in the dust.

"Nothing below the belt," he'd yell while he watched us practice his teachings on one another. But I liked to play dirty, hooking my legs around my sisters' legs when they least expected it and pinning them to the ground.

I was mad about everything ancient Greece. I poured over all the mythology books at the library. I obsessed over the family drama, memorized both the Greek and Roman names of the pantheon, and staged plays with my sisters of the various love triangles and sordid affairs between gods and men. It was all so absurd, so romantic. It was all so unbelievable. Once the Cuckoo was properly fanned and fed, we performed enactments of these dramas for her entertainment. If she laughed, a sign of success, she shared her candy. One single chocolate apiece which we were instructed to hold on our tongues until it melted. Torture and a test. A yawn from her was a sign we were failing at our jobs as her court fools and that we should up the ante of our games. A good old-fashioned three-way mime of a Chaplin walk usually did the trick.

"All right, chickadees, time to clean up. Mama has to get to work. Be good and lock up." We watched as the dust cleared from her truck pulling out of our driveway before walking to the diner for orange sodas and to watch reruns of the Star Theater Show. The television was a small seven-inch encased in walnut with horrible reception. If anyone moved—an outright guarantee in a diner—the picture would fuzz, pop, and fade. All the patrons would leap out of their booths, leave their eggs to get cold, their malts dripping down their chins, to shake their arms high in the air to bring the image back into focus. We made sure to only stay for one episode in order to beat Mama and Pop home so we could clean up our messes, not that they would have noticed anyway.

We always arrived just in time for *Sweet Tooth's Bakestravaganza Cooking Show and Sometimes Talk Show Show!* a sketch on the hour-long Star Theater Show. It opened with a shot of a staged kitchen. The counter, fridge, stove, and sink all faced front. Passersby floated along in the window over the sink. At the counter sat a young woman with a grey wig cut short, wearing very small round glasses and an all black outfit, with a typewriter, facing the screen. To her left sat the star puppet, Sweet Tooth. She had a potbelly and beanpole legs, messy yarn hair, a crazed look in her eyes, and a long spiked rock candy teeth hanging in an overbite from her drooling mouth. To the woman's right was Dust Bunny, a piece of lint with googly eyes. As the screen focused, Sweet Tooth licked a spoon with buttercream frosting with her felt tongue extended and flopping against the icing. Dust Bunny looked over the young woman's shoulder, his neckless head twisting mechanically like a barn owl's, as she stared blankly at her typewriter.

"Mmmhmmm buttercream frosting. I want to spread it all over monuments and public structures throughout the city. Like lampposts and statues and benches," said Sweet Tooth. "Ugh ugh ugh! This is going nowhere. Give me that spoon." The young woman grabbed the spoon and licked it.

"Hey! That's mine!" Sweet Tooth's claws unfurled. She scraped at the air near the young woman's face.

"You have to learn to share, Sweet Tooth." The woman fended off Sweet Tooth's scratches with the stick end of the spoon.

"Now, now you two, next time ask when you want something," Dust Bunny said. This little piece of filth was the rational one of the show. He gave them both a look of admonishment and the strings pulled his hands to his hips. The woman handed Sweet Tooth the spoon.

"Here. Happy?"

Dust Bunny peered over the young woman's typewriter, trying to read over her shoulder. The woman blocked his view with the back of hand.

"What's next on the docket, dear?"

"I think...I think...I mean here she is, she's been standing up to her ankles in the lake for a good while now. I think she either dives in, or walks out? Don't you think?"

"Seems to me she should jump in if she's been waiting there for that long."

"You know what would be good with this? Sugared strawberries!" Sweet Tooth was everyone's favorite but mine. I liked Dust Bunny best. My two dum-dum sisters cheered when she showed up with a sack of powdered sugar.

Sweet Tooth began to pull mixing bowls and ingredients out from under the table. She pulled out a measuring cup and measured her ingredients. She let the ingredients pile above the rim of the cup. While she wasn't looking a hand in a black glove evened out the top.

"One cup sugar, one cup flour, one cup butter, one cup buttermilk, one cup strawberries, one cup cream. Six cups!"

"Six cups of coffee is what I need right now," the waitress behind the counter at the diner said. "Can't we watch something else? Something with a plot? How about a romance?" Minny shushed her and we went back to our enraptured state, sucked into the siren song of the TV screen.

On screen, Sweet Tooth frantically stirred the mixing bowl. Flour went all over the table, walls, and Sweet Tooth herself. The hand appeared again and wiped the screen free of residue. The fog of flour remained on set for the rest of the show, like the fog in some scary bog-creature movie

"The secret is not to mix too much, otherwise your biscuits get tough! For a moist biscuit only stir one, two, three, four, five, six, seven, eight times!

Fold your dough five times. One, two, three,

four, five!" Sweet Tooth punched the dough vio-
lently, shaking the whole table. Dust Bunny and the
young woman held on to the table for dear life.

"Punch your dough! Punch punch punch! Cut
your dough in circles or squares, but never never
ever twist!" Sweet Tooth lit a match and set the table on fire. "Oh, I forgot to mention, you should
be preheating your oven at 450 degrees Fahrenheit,
232.222 Celsius."

The table was engulfed in flames. The young
woman and Dust Bunny kept talking as they grabbed
at ropes hanging from the ceiling to pull themselves
up. A stagehand dressed as a fireman entered with a
glass container of foam and began to spray the table
with a fire extinguisher.

"Now, arrange your little shapes on a baking
sheet, lined with parchment paper. And put them
in the oven. Bake your biscuits for eleven minutes.
Do not over bake! Also, do not under bake. Bake
them perfectly!" Sweet Tooth pulled the seared tray
of burned biscuits from the flames, which were dying down thanks to the efforts of the fireman puppet
wrangler. Her lips were sluggishly pulled down bit-
by-bit, first forming a perfectly horizontal line across
her face and then drooping in an exaggerated dripping arch off her chin. The frown fell to the floor and
water filled her eyes from bottom to top. She used
the end of her dribbled lip to wipe her eye and keep
herself from blubbering.

"Normally they should be a golden brown.
Not a black brown... So let's see here..." She rifled
under the table. Dozens of gloved hands appeared

raising up tuning forks, forceps, magic wands, chemistry beakers, and other utensils useless for the occasion. Sweet Tooth finally pulled out a can of gold spray paint and sprayed the biscuits. "Ahhaha! Perfecto Mundo! Now, top with strawberries dipped in sugar and cream!"

Sweet Tooth served the biscuits, one to Dust Bunny, one to the woman, and ten to herself.

"*Yum*! These are biscuits fit for a king. If I don't say so myself."

"But you do say so yourself." The woman and Dust Bunny stopped their conversation and stared at the golden biscuits. Dust Bunny picked one up and examined it from all angles. He showed one to a hidden puppeteer who twisted the biscuit in their gloved hand. One side was charred, one side was still gooey with undercooked batter.

"Um, what were you asking? I lost track." The writer gnawed at the edge of a biscuit.

"I don't remember...something about the explanation of explanation. What is explanation?" Dust Bunny asked.

"That's a very good question. Explanation is to explain explaining."

"That sounds hard."

"You think the biscuits are too hard? Oh darn, I must have left them in the oven for eleven and a half minutes! Or did I over stir? I remember counting to fifteen precisely. Here, try them with more cream!" Sweet Tooth dumped a bowl of cream on Dust Bunny's uneaten biscuit.

"Thank you Sweet Tooth, these look...special."

"I think I need a break. I need to get up and move around. They say that helps," the writer said. She stood up and stretched.

"Fantastic! I couldn't agree more. Let's go for a walk."

Dust Bunny grabbed the woman's shoulders with his claws and lifted her away from the table. Sweet Tooth called after them.

"Hey! Are you going to eat these?"

After a pause Sweet Tooth's mouth opened wide and she shoved both biscuits inside, chomping in sloppy bites. The grotesquely childish words flew across the screen: SWEET TOOTH'S BAKESTRAV-AGANZA BAKING AND COOKING SHOW AND SOMETIMES TALK SHOW SHOW. The announcer gushed: "Tune in for next week's guest: Edgar, the world famous Coney Island Footlong Hot Dog. Now, give it up for our house band, Bobbi Egg-White and the Gum Wads!" The image cut to a stringy stick of a man with a guitar and three wads of gum at a set of drums, a bass, and a keyboard, respectively. The band played the theme song as the credits rolled. A janitor came on stage to clean the mess. The images faded out.

"Thank heavens that's over." The waitress changed the station to a soap.

It was not the best episode, but it was still very satisfying. Ah, well, it was time to go before the Cuckoo noticed we had been gone all day.

At home we had a radio for our babysitter. My favorite programs were what the Cuckoo called the "not until you're older" shows. When the Cuckoo was home, the radio would be on all day—a constant stream of twenty-four-hour stories and news. Our father's arrival home was met with the clicking off of the radio. He claimed the noise gave him a headache, that he couldn't think, and that he had enough static in his brain. When neither of them were home, we'd blast that radio as loud as it could go, playing music and dancing and shaking to bebop, or listening to those not-until-we-were-older shows.

Every year at Christmas time, our family would get in our jalopy and drive the two or so hours to see a real movie at a real movie theater. We went to the cheapest showing, so we only saw the out-of-date films. Thankfully our mother was just as mesmerized by celebrity mystique as we were and kept the house filled with a never-ending supply of gossip rags and a subscription to the weekly entertainment section of the newspaper. On Saturday mornings we'd run the half mile or so to the cluster of mailboxes at the edge of our trailer park. We stood in the blow-dried desert morning air already sweating while we waited for the day's delivery. When the mail truck crested that horizon line, we'd jump and howl just like the diner patrons trying to get the picture back on the TV, trying to get some focus. The game went like this: whoever caught the thick wad of mail from the postman got to read it out loud to the other two, before the Cuckoo woke up. Meanwhile, the two losers had to make everyone silver dollar pancakes. We snuck a bit of the Cuckoo's whisky in our orange juice concentrate to loosen it up.

Sometimes the Cuckoo left us in the care of our

neighbor Maggie. We looked enough like Maggie's own raven-haired daughter to trick her into feeding us before her own kin. Her house was about the size of a wooden post and we had to squeeze ourselves even more to fit inside. I have fond memories of days spent with Maggie in the back of her station wagon on the way to the ice rink. Maggie would wake us up with bowls of cornflakes and pull our hair into tight French braids. We spent the day with migraines from the wear and tear on our scalps. To placate us during car rides she gave us pink pistachios that we used to stain our lips crimson so we could make kissy faces at the passing cars.

At the skating rink we ordered all the flavors from the flavored ice man and called the concoction hubby bubby. Esther was a natural at skating. She won the hokey-pokey and the limbo every Saturday, beating out all the seasoned skaters. If our destination was the theater, we brought penny candy and threw it at the back of patrons' heads. On the car rides home, Maggie would tune the radio to a serial about a ship captain lost at sea. I imagined the disembodied voice as my Father's when he left, as though he flew into the radio and spoke to us in airwaves.

"Girls, pay attention. This show will teach you about survival and wit. Not that you three don't already have too much gumption for your own good," Maggie said.

The show opened with the same sounds every week: the sounds of the sea. A creaking ship. A hiss. Water leaking in drips. Then a soothing man's voice would appear. His stories and inflection would send my sisters and us to our afternoon naps.

"Ay me. There isn't much else more soothing than the sound of the sea. Perhaps the sound of a good woman humming, or onions sautéing on the stove. Oh, to have a bit of cast-ironed food—a steak, some chicken livers, a spoon bread pudding... I've had nothin' but raw food for six weeks, ever since the gas ran out. Unless you count the little bit o' cookin' that happens naturally from the heat of the sun. Such as leavin' a fish out to bake. If we burn in the sun, why not fish flesh? I can't complain though, being out here, free, doin' what I love best: Bein' on a ship."

The man's voice was more like vibrations than speech. I felt a yawn coming on. More sounds of the scraping a knife, whittling, and a knife against metal.

"Yup, I love bein' away from it all—the stress, the crowds, the obligations. On a ship your only obligation is movin' one thing, or two things, or people, or persons, from one place to another. You're following a path and enjoying the ride. You're steering your favorite lady through adventurous waters." He paused and there again were the sounds of sea, a creaking ship, a hiss, and water leaking.

"Of course, like anyone, I'm apt to miss certain things. But out here, you can *really* think. You can excavate your mind. There isn't much else to do, after all! You can really get in your own head. You can think about what you could have done differently, all those missed opportunities... Heck! You can even finish the arguments you never finished, say what you really wanted to say. No one is gonna stop ya. We're used to talkin' aloud to ourselves out here." I was the last to close my eyes to the Captain and his sinking ship.

Our trailer was parked near a river named the Saint Good Journey. Some folk called it the Prairie Hen. Calling it a river at all was misleading. Most of the year the river was all mud. In the heat the Cuckoo would brave the slop, claiming it cooled and cleansed her body. She'd emerge covered to her ears with filth and chase us around, threatening us with hugs. Minny and Esther took a shine to bathing in the muddy river as well, showing off their handstands underwater while I walked the perimeter of the shore, occasionally tipping my toe in the edge. We collected heron shit from the river and performed spells to turn the turds into diamonds for a better year ahead, a more fortunate year. We sat at the river's edge pretending it was the ocean—a thing we'd never seen so had nothing to measure what we imagined against. To us, a murky pit was as marvelous as la mer. We lounged in hand-me-down bathing suits that sagged in the butt and at the breasts, all the elastic spent on bigger bodies. We used our hands, balled into loose fists with loops made from our thumbs and pointer fingers to simulate binoculars, scanning the sky for incoming foreign objects.

"I think I see something," I had an active imagination.

"What? Where?"

"I don't see anything. Just some kids splashing around," Minny took the bait.

"That! There! You see that?"

"What? Where?"

"That! That thing! That thing in the water! What is that?"

"Is it a shark?"

"Don't say that so loud! You'll start a panic."

"Well, if it is a shark, we should be panicking."

"No, it's not a shark. It's some sort of ... bird."

"You mean a gull? That's a normal sight at a beach, sis."

"No! Not a gull. It's brighter, downright ... tropical."

"Trop-i-what?"

"Tropical. Of, or relating to, the tropical zone, i.e. below the equator, i.e., hot as hell. You know, technically, I think we're living in a subtropic zone this time of year."

"I don't see anything. Here, give me those." Esther grabbed my hands and used them on her own eyes for a better view. "Hm ... I don't ... I see it! I see what you mean! There! It's big, real big."

"Yes! You see, I'm not crazy. Does it have red tail feathers?"

"Yes! Red tail feathers but otherwise all black. Man, that's a big bird."

"Don't tell me it's a red-tailed black cockatoo!"

"Those are very rare! I've never seen one be-fore." And now Esther grabbed my hands and placed them over her eyes. "Let me see!"

We stayed out there on the banks of that river from sunrise to sunset. We'd oil up with canola and pack a basket of crackers and salami, sometimes a thermos full of the Cuckoo's coconut flavored hooch. At sundown we moseyed home, drained from the sun and the hard work of being a look-out.

In our small front yard we kept a lame horse also named Pearl. One day I got it into my head to make a new moon to hang in the sky by mixing glue made from her hooves with the buried heron shit. On a recent trip to the museum I learned that anti-venom is made from stabbing a horse with infected needles until a resistance is built up, so I figured I could extract some practical medicine. I found a knife in the kitchen large enough to get the job done and approached the sleeping old mare, careful not to spook her with sudden movement.

"Here Pearly Pearl, I'm not going to hurt you." I pinned the knife to the back of my shirt with one hand, and extended my other toward her, palm up, just like our father taught us to do when meeting a new animal. She let me stroke her flank and mane. She nuzzled into me and I distracted her with a handful of oats from my pocket. I thought I only had to extract the glue from the hooves like tapping a tree for sap. I carved Pearl's left heel and she made a noise that penetrated the earth, causing a deep rumble below me, a tragic vibration to the dearly departed. She tried to stand but her wounded leg buckled beneath her and her body swayed toward mine. She gnashed at me with her teeth and pushed me to the ground with her back leg, knocking the wind out of me. Her old body couldn't withstand the pain, the wound turned to a volcano, the blood parting her as lava would and congealing with the chaparral of the dry river bed. By the time I got my wind back, and was able to cry for help, Pearl had eroded in all directions, cleaving to the earth.

We buried the mare under the elm tree at the center of the trailer park. My mother stood by while I dug the grave and sang a eulogy.

> *The mare, fair Queen of Scots, enjuste*
> *a rightful heir was she.*
> *But as e'er time did not align*
> *with stars, nor will of queen.*
>
> *Whose truth is true and whose untrue?*
> *These stories will abound.*
> *A plot, a death, a murderous coup*
> *no alibis are sound.*
>
> *The mare begs for mercy, please!*
> *I'll change my devious ways!*
> *But cries fall on deaf ears,*
> *twas time to end her days.*
>
> *And so, our mare, our rightful queen*
> *was placed in our humble home*
> *and bestowed a job of little skill*
> *with birds and other crones.*

Mama gave a speech about life as a series of endless falling. She said: "It starts with the hole we dig from here to China when we're young and dumb. In and out of this and that, maybe to nothing, but most times to something, a somewhere we stay in for only a moment. Then the hole we dug opens up again and we continue to fall in circles forever and ever and ever. Amen."

Esther and Minny stepped in to help when they saw me struggling to dig a hole deep enough to contain the carcass of the horse. Where we dug the hole we found a fossilized calf, a stillborn. Another sister? My head ached, a migraine brought on by those French braids. This one was like ice shooting through the maze of my brain. I remembered the story of Athena from the library's mythology book. Her debut on earth was a victorious burst through the top of Zeus's skull. Women give birth to the fleshy and messy and loud parts of humanity through small slits. If mortal men were to give birth, life would come out as concepts, clean and clear. I imagined myself with a daughter, but the image disappeared.

At Pearl's funeral, my sisters and I kicked up her remains alongside tar, dust, and fool's gold from the ground. We danced around one another and though I hadn't made a new moon, we discovered we could contort ourselves into crescents. Our childhood was forever preserved in the burial mound, and our futures were arranged into voids, debts, and gifts.

SNAKE OIL

The day we met Bette it was unusually cool in the desert and the sagebrush was tinged with unseasonable morning frost. It was a few months before our sixteenth birthday, a very important year, we were told. To the north, the sky was clear as crystal. To the south, dark storm clouds masked the sun, infusing the town with an ominous affectation. It was Independence Day and most everything was shut down to prepare for the annual fireworks show, save for the Little Bad and the movie theater, the only businesses that stayed open every day of the year.

"Holidays are some of our biggest money-making days," said the theater owner, a decrepit old man named Noah.

But Noah didn't know how to choose his features, showing out-of-date films on repeat. How many times could a person watch *Gone with the Wind* in one week? Our record was three. I loved determined, ruthless, and manipulative Scarlett O'Hara. She was a real go-getter, and a beauty to boot. She taught me that when life burns your curtains, you make them into a dress. I loved that film from start to finish but even I couldn't watch Atlanta burning more than five times in a row. The fireworks weren't scheduled to shoot until sundown so we had time to kill. When there's a to-do in the sticks, everyone who is able shows up. And so it was that there was an outdoor exodus in little Sandpiper Springs to see a traveling medicine show.

Earlier that week this kid from school had told me that a medicine show was coming to town for the holidays. We were practicing our time tables together—I was a bright child, excelling in all my classes. I read at a level five years advanced for my age. I recited the multiplication tables in a breeze, won the spelling bee with words like "penultimate" and "vivisepulture." Therefore, I was assigned to mentor what the school called "a Twinkling Tot"—a kid who was falling behind in his lessons. This kid told me that a medicine show was all voodoo and magical cures and freak shows with multiple heads, eyes, tails, and humans taller than any building in Sandpiper Springs and fatter than a double-wide.

He said last year his aunt was on her deathbed with The Fever when all the color of her eyes had turned pale pink. He said his mother saw her sister's spirit start to float away when she remembered the magic elixir she bought from a traveling quack a few months back in a town just over the border. She hurried to her bedside drawer and forced the liquid from the vial into her sister's mouth. He said she said she saw her sister's spirit struggling to let go. But then, his aunt's body animated and grabbed hold tightly to her sister's neck. As the liquid performed its job—over an agonizing hour in which his mom's neck was wrung thin—his aunt's spirit was tacked back into her body and, thus, she was revitalized. After one more day of bed rest, the kid said, she was back at work in the fields and sewing curtains and making the best beef stew in the county—besides his mother's, of course.

It didn't take much to convince me. I was craving something stimulating to get things moving, rile me up, and my mind was as malleable as my joints. So, when I told my sisters I wanted to resurrect Pearl (I was, by then, supposed to be repenting for my sins) and that our Saturday would be spent with the rest of town at this just-passing-through miracle show, we all gathered to see what cures were at hand.

The whole of Sandpiper Springs was on that trail, journeying on a meditative walk through sameness. Our landscape was repetition: a flat trail cycling over and over, even past the horizon line. The medicine show was parked at the top of town, where granite formed mountains and Joshua trees lifted their arms up in reverence to the gods of the sky. We arrived on time but there was already a crowd. We jumped to see the stage but eventually decided it was best to use our small size to our advantage and crawl, on hands and knees, to make our way to the front and center.

On stage was a woman with a violin and two ballerinas frozen in fifth position on either side of the platform. One was dressed in all black, the other in all white. The violinist played the third act of *Swan Lake* as the ballerinas began to mock fight. They weren't graceful like my father. That man could deliver a one-two knockout before you saw it coming. You'd think he was handing you a bouquet and bam! you were on your butt with your legs in the air, seeing those much talked about stars. These women fought spitefully, the way I fought with my sisters—dirty, nasty, pulling at hair, and full of animalistic rage. I looked to my left, Esther was bewitched. She was tapping out time with her fingertips. To my right, Minny was also frozen in concentrated awe, her arms tucked across her chest. Tick tick tick, I could hear her taking mental notes. I tried to read her mind to cheat for words. I too fixed my gaze on these two dancing comediennes. Never in my life had I seen anything so engaging, true, and funny.

While the two women were entangled in a fallen brawl—a headlock, as my father would call it—out from behind the curtain emerged the most handsome man that I had ever seen. He was wearing a perfectly tailored suit the color of mallard feathers, an iridescent green-blue-black. He wore a jet-black top hat, covering what we saw as slicked-back raven's hair. His shoes were shined so they reflected the sun in our eyes, blinding us momentarily. He wore luminescent makeup around his eyes to match his suit.

Oh!

The two ballerinas did a pas de deux to meet him in the middle of the stage and then continued their fight. This time, they dueled for his affection and attention, pushing and pulling his arms. Try the old hook-around-the-knee, I thought. But this match was too choreographed for a sneak attack. The peacock was relaxed, calm, and unaffected. He smiled. He eventually took them both by the arm and tucked them close to his side. He kissed them each on the cheek and they seemed satisfied. The audience heaved a sigh of relief.

All was well!

"Ladies and gentlemen!" he announced strutting around the platform.

"Ladies and gentlemen," he repeated in a high falsetto.

Something was off with the register of the man's voice. This timbre did not belong to this body. This voice was buttery and soft, unlike any man's voice I had heard before. My father had a husky crow, my math teacher Mr. Butro spoke through his nose, and the man on the radio talked as deep as my voice sounded when I screamed from the bottom of the river. The peacock removed his top hat and shook a long mane of black hair to his waist. The audience gasped. He's a She! This woman was a tall and graceful creature with all the extended features of a crane. My sisters and I squeezed each other's hands and stifled quiet screams of delight.

"Ladies and Gentlemen, my name is Bette Bunting. To my left is Odette, to my right is Odile—not their given names, of course. Together we make up three-fifths of the Bette Bunting Cardinal Five Revue. We're just passing through your lovely little desert town on the last leg of our coastal tour. Yes, we were just passing through and thought, gosh darn it, how can we not stop here at this beautiful place? We came all the way from way up in northern California, deep in the redwoods, ladies and gentlemen. We're all itching to get home but we just couldn't resist stopping by your gorgeous little village. Yes, we drove past and were entranced. Now *we're* here to entrance *you*, ladies and gentlemen! There's no cost, no cost, this show is completely free. We do all this in the hope that one day you will return the favor and visit us in our dear home in the redwoods. Now, you may be asking, Bette, you said Cardinal Five, but there are only two bodies on stage. What gives? Well! The other three are at home resting from a turkey feast—gravy isn't the best for dancing, sorry to say—so this is merely a taste of what you'd usually find up there!

"Ballet? You scoff. En pointe not quite your taste? What else can we do, you ask? What other tricks are up our sleeves? What else do we offer? Entertainment my dear friends, pure, unbridled entertainment. We aren't like those other traveling shows, offering miracle cures for leprosy or blindness, no ma'ams, no sirs. Hear me out. There ain't no better cure for what ails you than entertainment, in my humble opinion. Morphine, pills, tonics, elixirs, those will only get you so far, trust me, and not to mention all those nasty side effects. We're addictive but not the kind of addiction that wrestles into your bones, ladies and gentlemen! There are no side effects here except possible stitches in your side or a lifelong dedication to the stage! We have fire eaters, mind readers, dancers, and singers. We have jugglers, comics, and theater. And the best part? We're all easy on the eyes.

"And me? What do I do, since I'm not here to hawk some quack wares, you ask? Well, my role is to be like the sheepdog, you see. I find talent and inspiration and shepherd it, my friends. I take schemes and dreams and make them happen. And then I present it for folks like you. Now, you may have heard some folk call me a witch, but those folk are small-minded, let me tell you. What I do is, yes, a sort of magic, but not the dark sort. It's basic alchemy, my friends. I combine equal parts beautiful performers, innate talent, with a little business savvy, et voilà! We have ourselves a show worth your time."

Bette stooped low, met my eyes and said:

"I can't bring back your sister."

She rose again, craned her neck high, and addressed the entire audience:

"I can't help you win the jackpot, or get rid of that nagging mother-in-law, I can't help your crops grow verdant and be prosperous this summer. But! My girls and I can help you forget about all those heavy burdens for about an hour-and-a-half. Just an hour-and-a-half of your time, an hour-and-a half spent away from the responsibilities, the toil, the whining kids. Whatever it is that ails you. All right, all right, I'm sure y'all are sick of my pitch by now. So let's get started, eh? We'll do one more quick routine, and hit the road, what do you say?"

The black and white swans did another pas de deux to the center of the stage. When they met, they crashed into one another and each one fell to the ground. They were accompanied by an adagio beat from the violinist. They then exited the stage and returned holding two large cardboard packing boxes. They climbed in the boxes and, from the inside, began to speak.

"Hello? Anyone out there? Can anyone hear me? I locked myself in. I let the door close behind me—I think the heat made it expand and now it's stuck. Hello? Oh. I think that's the neighbor boy, Colin. Colin! Up here. Oh I don't think he can hear me," the voice from the box on the left said.

"Here, let me try this: I'll toss something out the window and see if it gets his attention," said box number two.

"Who are you?! Where'd you come from?!" Box one.

"I've been here all along. You didn't see me? I've been right beside you the entire time." Box two.

"Are you sure? I certainly didn't notice...."

"What do you mean, 'Am I sure?' Of course I'm sure!"

"Calm down, calm down. Now is not the time to get worked up. We're in this together now, whether we were in it together from the start or not."

"There is no 'or not.'"

"Pardon? You're asking me to decide between 'no' and 'not?' That's a tough one. 'No' implies another choice I am denying, and only one other choice. That being 'yes.' And 'not,' well 'not' implies that there are many other choices, or that there could be many other choices, or just one, you can't be sure. 'Not' could also be a state of mind or being, I am 'not' this or 'not' that but it doesn't necessarily mean I am something else entirely, either. 'Not' feels more open. I choose 'not!'"

"What in the world are you talking about?"

"You were asking me about the existence of 'no' and 'not.'"

"No, no, I believe you misheard me. I was telling you there is no 'or not' pertaining to my being here earlier with you. Before you noticed me. Because quite certainly I was here. So it's a resounding 'Yes, I was here.'"

"Well, I'm glad. Two heads are better than one."

"How did you know I have two heads?"

"I ... it's an expression. You have two heads?"

"It's a riddle, what creature has two heads and one tail?"

"A gryphon?"

"No, no, think again. A real creature."

"I haven't a clue."

"A human holding a penny! A penny, you see, has one head and one tail. And a human has one head. Adding up to two heads and one tail." The box shifted slightly from the enthusiasm of the figure hidden inside.

"Oh! Brilliant! Tell me another! I love riddles!"

"I'm afraid that's the only riddle I know."

"Oh well. Life's enough of a puzzle, eh? Say, are you a gambling man?" Box two spoke low this time. The crowd leaned in undivided to better hear the words, causing the earth to shift ever so slightly toward the stage.

"Yes, I love all games. Vingt-et-un is my favorite."

"Good, shall we play vingt-et-un to pass the time?"

"Time isn't passing and it won't pass. It simply is. This present becomes my past and that past becomes my present. And so forth. Like a carousel or a cuckoo in a cuckoo clock. There will always be a one am every day and a two am and a three am and so forth."

"Round and round, I see what you mean. Do you still want to play vingt-et-un?"

"Yes! I'll shuffle and deal."

The sound of shuffling cards and dealing was audible through the boxes.

"Hm, hit me."

"I'll take one too."

"You can't look at what you're taking! Besides the One card is the best card!"

"No no, I'm taking *a* card, as well. Not THE One card."

"Oh, sorry, I understand. Sorry for getting worked up. I just take all games very seriously."

They paused. I looked around to see if anyone was laughing. They were all in stitches! I, however, found the humor simple. I thought to myself, *My father is funnier than you. My sisters are much funnier, too.*

"Would you like another card?"

"Yes, please, hit me."

"I'm holding."

"Me as well."

"Show your hand."

The two voices in the box were silent for a very long time. The sun began to set and twilight settled to the earth. Mosquitos appeared and nipped at my calves.

"What do I have? I can't see. Did I win?" Box number one broke the pause.

"Hm, didn't think of that. I can't see either. Let's call it a draw!"

"Deal! Good game, good game. Shall we play another round?"

The two women jumped out from the boxes, tipped their hats, fanned the cards into the audience and restarted their brawl. They mimed fisticuffs and tumbled into the final five minutes of *Swan Lake*. Both dancers died in somersaults off the stage. The laughing crowd was a herd in a hysterical state, lemmings in stitches tumbling off an edge into the absurd. I could hardly breathe from all the laughing. My exhalations were not met accordingly with my inhalations. *If I die laughing*, I thought, *that'll be a fine way to go*.

Bette re-emerged wiping tears from her smiling eyes.

"Oh, I have the most talented women in my revue, wouldn't you agree, ladies and gentlemen? Now you'll just have to make that short trek up north to see the rest of us in our proper home! But ladies and gentlemen, I'm ashamed to say I failed to mention our plight here tonight. Because we were so enraptured by your town, because of its surreal beauty, we so had to stop. We went out of our way, off the planned path of our coastal tour, and spent the rest of our gas money on this glorious detour! It was worth it, let me promise you, but now we have no money to get home to Sky-on-the-Lake, back to our own families and obligations. So I'm here now, asking for any donations, anything you can give, to help us on our journey. If you have nothing, it was worth it. You are the best audience this side of the Colorado and Sandpiper Springs is our new favorite town! We'll surely put this place on our map for the next year's tour. Anything at all, any donation large or small, is appreciated, so appreciated, God give thanks."

The black and white swans stepped into the audience and walked around with upturned top hats to collect our donations. The entire town emptied their pockets. This was surprising since Sandpiper Springs was infamous for its cheapskates. The richest doctor in town was known to dip his hand in the charity food bin, stuffing cans of creamed corn in his coat pockets. The sky had turned completely dark and glittering silver lights were falling to the earth. I looked down and my feet were frozen solid. My lips, and the lips of my brethren, were ice blue as well.

"This is better than church," Minny said.

Everyone threw the contents of their wallets and purses intact into the upturned hats. When the black swan reached my sisters and me, we, ashamed, had only penny candy to offer. The black swan looked at the penny candy, then at us with a penetrating gaze. She reached into her hat and gave us each a silver dollar, a fortune for us.

She left, but not before grabbing our candy and taking a violent bite.

After the swans had collected money from all the townsfolk, they flitted off the stage. They broke their set down in mere moments and disappeared to their trailer. Their caravan took off, rambling through dust and bumping down the flat road from Sandpiper Springs to the north. The storm clouds parted and night came in its usual way. The audience's feet thawed and we all scattered in a daze, murmuring about what we thought we had seen to one another. My sisters and I walked the six miles home radiant and gushing. *Did you see! Can you imagine! Oh how I'd love to perform!*

When we got home, we placed our silver dollars under our mattress.

"Just like the Princess and the Pea," Esther mused.

"Let's hope this turns to riches," Minny said.

We three fell asleep quickly and deeply that night, each having no dreams at all but vague feelings of a chill. We had forgotten about the fireworks.

By the end of that summer, Pop flew off on one of his jobs with his collection of tiny ships and this time didn't return. We waited for days, then weeks, and a then months for presents but they, and he, never came.

"Who needs him?" the Cuckoo said. "All we need is our feral female family." His leaving wouldn't be the knockout punch, but without what little support and stability he provided, Mama's stance did waver. The Little Bad's manager had racked up quite the gambling debt and leveraged the building to his bookies. The new owners remodeled the bar to attract bigger names and fired all the local amateur billings, including the Cuckoo. With her wheelhouse crumbled, and no allegiance to us, she took off for who knows where. We stayed awake listening to her mark time over a bottle and then the deep beats of her diesel truck as it crawled slowly down our gravel path just before the sun was starting to rise.

Our neighbor Maggie balked at the county when asked if she wanted to foster the three of us until we found permanent homes. She had two kids of her own, for chrissakes. It was one thing to feed us plain noodles and drive us to the skating rink on Saturday mornings. It was another to pay for schooling, clothes, and lessons of varying kinds, thrice over.

My sisters and I were tight as a thicket, and none of us dumb. We were skinny girls with dirt on our faces fleeing toward uncertain futures, piloting the darkness. The day the county was supposed to pick us up we packed a duffel bag with overnight clothes, toothbrushes, and baking soda, tins of butter biscuits, and a change of underwear. We took the "Mexico Fund" money the Cuckoo hid behind her shoes in the closet as bus fare. At the depot we were puzzled by the colored lines that made up the map of bus routes. East, West, North, or South? *East is east and West is west / And the wrong one I have chose.* The names of the towns meant nothing to us, save one: Sky-on-the-Lake.

"Those women, those traveling ballerinas said their troupe was from up north, near Sky-on-the-Lake. Maybe they need some new talent?" Minny said.

For seven hours we rode from the tedious beauty of the desert to the lush redwood forest. Minny and Esther cuddled and giggled on a shared bench while I pretended to sleep on a single seat. I tried to forget my fears, to take in the pine and ocean, not to worry about money or to curse the Cuckoo. High and dry and deserted. I was searching the sky out my window when I saw that bird again, the strange tropical creature far from home.

"Did you hear that? That squawk? I think that bird is back!"

"You know Ms. Tenniel in Lot 72B? She had twelve zebra finches?"

"Twelve zebra finches in that tiny trailer?"

"Zebra finches are very rare."

"No wonder they're disappearing, Ms. Tenniel of Sandpiper Springs Trailer Park is hoarding them all."

"She had an umbrella cockatoo, too!"

"Cockatoo, too!"

"Cockatoo, too! Cockatoo, too!"

"Shhhh! I'm trying to hear! You don't hear that cooing?"

"That was us."

"No, no, I'm not an idiot. I heard this loud noise coming from the break water, over there."

"Over where? There can be anywhere when you're pointing at the sea," Esther grabbed my binocular hands.

"What does it sound like, Pearly?"

"It sounds like ... coo, coo, cool, cool!"

"Cool! Cool!" Esther and Minny were now shouting out the window. The other passengers were shifting in annoyance in their seats and hiding behind newspapers.

"Wait, no. It's not cool. It's cruel!"

"Cruel! Cruel!"

"Stop it! Listen."

They cupped their ears: listening. I leaned into their hands, c-shaped, and screamed:

"HERE BIRDIE BIRDIE!"

"Would you three pipe down!" The bus driver was now yelling at us in the rearview mirror.

I put my fake binoculars down and made my hands into muzzles for my two squawking sisters who were throwing obscenities at me and calling me the cruel one now. *Cruel cruel cruel,* they crowed at me. The other people on the bus were grateful for my hushing, too, I could tell.

The towns we passed were cartoon caricatures of highway hamlets: flat front buildings, solitary trucks moving down distant roads, coffee shops with the World's Best Coffee. The monochromatic palette of the scene suited my mood—dull, yet precise. I was used to the shades of auburn terra cotta on the main drag of Sandpiper Springs. Natural pools of water glimmered in the twilight. New power lines weaved in and out like spider webs. There was so much stillness. In all that placidity I thought of the half-humans from my mythology book—centaurs, satyrs, and chimera—who, with fearsome limbs, would gallop across the silence.

At each station stop, Esther, Minny, and I sprinted up and down the track, desperate for exercise. I found the northern part of the state eerie, the low-level fog loomed at our ankles while wolves howled at a full moon that took up the whole sky.

I had watched too many monster movies, creatures from the Black Lagoon, aliens from Mars, chthonic blobs and such, to know better than to linger like sitting ducks in a town that was ripped from those storylines.

"We have to go now," I told my sisters. "This place gives me the willies."

Minny and Esther, always game for a touch of drama, feigned being spooked and rushed back to the bus to huddle in their seats.

"That town is haunted," Minny said.

"I'm sure of it," Esther said.

❋

I woke from a nap to the sound of the bus pulling into a gravel parking lot. The driver announced the end the line. He heaved his massive body toward the general store and returned to lean against the side of the bus with a thin stick of meat and a fountain soda.

"I thought this bus went up all the way to Sky-on-the-Lake?" Minny asked him.

"This is as far as we're going this time," he said.

"Where are we supposed to stay?"

"Plenty of motels open this time of year. Lucky for you, it's the off season."

But we were strapped for cash and knew better than to put our names down in a motel ledger. We walked up the highway, where we saw a sign for a nature preserve camping site, for two dollars a night, with toilets and outdoor cooking supplies.

"Where are your folks?" the ranger asked when we asked for a lot.

"They'll be along shortly," Minny said. "They sent us ahead to secure a site before they all get snatched up. They're in town buying supplies."

We bought a pound of halibut from a fisherman down at the monger's dock with the rest of our bus money. There was a communal barbecue on the grounds but we thought it best to fashion our own temporary fire pit, so as not to draw attention to ourselves. Minny was the one who got the fire going strong. The fish was fresh from the sea that morning, the flesh like silk on my tongue. After our meal we picked our teeth of the brittle bones and fell asleep by the fire. In the morning we snuck down to where the hiking trail met the beach to forage for mussels. On our way back we picked miner's lettuce. As we were boiling water to cook our breakfast, the ranger of the preserve approached us and told us we had to get going.

"Sorry girls, I can't be abetting minors," he said. "Here, take your two dollars back and here—some milk buns from my wife."

We packed what little we had and walked to town, nibbling on the day-old bread.

"What now?" I asked my sisters.

"I can't eat these heels and I'm starved, let's stop in here," Esther said, pointing at a restaurant up a set of wooden stairs.

We took a booth by the window overlooking the bay. Minny fiddled with the mini jukebox and chose a ragtime diddy. Esther groaned.

"This song again?"

Minny wriggled in her seat to the tune and ignored the de-harmonized pleas of our sister until the three of us fell into a perfect-pitch rendition, complete with tabletop acrobatics.

We ordered a tall stack of pancakes to share plus one whole sundae each. All with whip cream, all with rainbow sprinkles, two with fudge, and one with butterscotch.

"How do you suppose we get to Sky-on-the-Lake from here? We've used up all our money." Minny drenched the stack with maple syrup. She carved

the pile into perfect thirds and served Esther and me
our shares. My sisters made to dig in but I remind-
ed them that we were grownups now and grownups
had manners. They poised themselves and we ate in
silence with mindful etiquette, holding our fork and
knives properly and pausing between chews. Despite
our best efforts, the table was coated with crumbs
and half-used pats of melted butter.

"Anything else, or you girls ready to settle
up?" the waitress asked, clearing our sloppy mess.
She laid all three plates and all three bowls on her
right arm, and piled the utensils, nine in all, onto the
top plate, not once dropping a crumb or making any
clanging sounds.

Esther sniffled and her voice wavered. She
twirled her disheveled curls. Minny and I took the
cue—we set our eyes solemnly to our hands folded
in our laps.

"Ma'am, we came up here to visit our sick
aunt and she just passed this morning. We spent all
our money just to get up here and she didn't have a
penny to her name neither."

The waitress ripped off a ticket from her pad
and slid it toward us.

"You can pay at the front."

"Now you've done it, Esther."

"Me? What'd I do?"

"It was your choice to come in here in the first
place."

"It's worked before! They must be extra stingy
up here!"

"Well, time to make a break for it then," I said.

"I see what y'all are up to," the waitress said, returning to our table. "But there's no need, that woman there took care of your bill. Now get out of here."

Seated at the counter was the mallard woman from the Fourth of July performance, Bette Bunting. She sat reading the newspaper over a bowl of bran flakes. She smiled at us and motioned for us to come sit next to her on the swivel seats.

"You girls are quite the team. But your performance needs work. Say, don't I recognize you from somewhere?"

"We're from Sandpiper Springs, ma'am. Your troupe stopped through our town, remember?"

"Oh that godforsaken place. We broke down there, now I remember. What are you doing all the way up here?"

"We're visiting our sick aunt."

"Don't give me that, I make a living off performers. I know when someone's acting. What are you really doing up here?"

"We had nowhere to go. We remembered you were from a town called Sky-on-the-Lake and we picked it off a map. We liked the name."

"It is indeed a name with implications. Where are your parents?"

"Gone, ma'am."

"It's Bette, not ma'am. What do you mean gone?"

"Gone."

"Adios."

"Flown the coop."

"Sayonara."

"Bye-bye."

"I see. And where will you be staying in Sky-on-the-Lake? Don't tell me this sick aunt left a mansion for you?"

"No ma'am, Bette. We got kicked out of our spot."

"Well, in that case you don't have much to lose. It wouldn't be right if I let three girls spend the night alone in a strange town. The nights get cool up here this time of year, you know? I like your bravado, and your little song-and-dance act. Why don't you girls come with me, you can spend the night at the theater and we'll find a way for you to thank me in the morning."

Bette finished her bowl of cereal in great sloppy bites and left a fat tip on the counter. She corralled us into the back of a polished convertible parked at an angle in the lot. She climbed in through the top, rather than opening her door.

"Buckle up!" She drove fast and recklessly, passing cars on the left and the right, shouting words back to us that we could not hear over the wind. We arrived at her place with ice cream melted down our chins, elbows, and shirt cuffs, and rainbow confetti stuck in our teeth.

CANARIES

Bette's girls performed and lived in a former hotel—a dilapidated clapboard Victorian with a wraparound porch painted with a fresh coat of ruby red. The building and its goings-on were a sore thumb in the little town by the bay. She had taken the lease over from her family and what was once a sleepy family estate was now a raucous stop-over for ne'er-do-wells. The townsfolk scoffed at everything out of the ordinary: vacationers, TV dinners, even water from the tap. So when Bette rolled in and announced her plans to turn the old Bunting hotel into a live performance hall, well it caused a miniature scandal that rippled through each day via nosy neighbors, noise complaints, and phone calls to the sheriff. Still, many of the townsfolk came for Bette's shows out of "curiosity," claiming disinterest but still making up a good percentage of ticket sales.

Bette ran a tight ship. She censored all the acts until they were pure inoffensive fluff. And she forbade romance with audience members. Bette had hit on a black hole in the variety show circuit: the sleepy town where options for entertainment were slim-to-none. What's more, Sky-on-the-Lake was full of folks who had trained for a foreign invasion, or men on voyages for gold or land, holding on to promises that never came, eager for a way to release all their pent-up punch.

"I dreamed once of traveling to Chicago and New York. We would work defunct medicine shows, dime stores, saloons, and legit theaters up and down the coast. I want more people to see what I have to offer, and see what my girls have to offer, too. But, for now, I am the queen of the northern coast variety show scene, and that's no small peanuts." Bette opened the fence, a ramshackle picket border with disintegrating paint that left soft splinters in my hand.

A path was formed by a set of large rocks embedded in the earth—our red carpet arrival. The front door was a behemoth of stained glass with a gargantuan doorknob that required a two-hand grip. The windows that faced the street were also made of extravagant stained glass in an abstract pattern of shapes and colors. A bay window at the top was painted over with white and red diamond stenciling.

We, and any visitors to the show, were welcomed through an elaborate receiving parlor. The floor was covered corner-to-corner by a Persian rug with a weeping willow design. Wingback chairs were set around the edge and a small electric fountain trickled running water. Bette kept fresh rose hips in large art deco vases on an austere wall-length credenza. One small chandelier hung from the ceiling shedding inadequate light. It was the middle of the day when we arrived but the interior was so insulated by luscious fabrics and furniture, and the light was so filtered by the colored glass windows, it could have been midnight for all we knew. From the outside, the house looked like your typical Victorian, but inside the rooms expanded into the proportions of a palace.

In the Saint Good Journey River trailer I had dreamed of a titanic house with rooms laid out in a circle separated by broad thresholds I could run through like a racetrack, rather than a set of closed square cubes. This was the kind of house that raised people of import, a stronghold capable of housing the high-octane gods of Olympus.

Seated in the parlor was a zaftig beauty with ebony hair tumbling down to her back. She looked young but put on airs, so she could have been twenty-one or forty-one.

"Girls, this is Blanca, she'll show you around. Blanca is our knife expert and fire eater. Blanca these are the Starlings, they'll be staying with us for a while."

"Nice to meet you." She extended her hand and smiled, revealing crooked and snaggled teeth. Her hand was slick with lotion.

Blanca led us to the back of the parlor through a ceiling-to-floor-length curtain leading to the entertainment room. Bette had replaced all the old wood floors with chic black-and-white speckled marble. A bar placed in the center of the room was lined with all shapes and sizes of bottles containing liquors in all the colors of the rainbow and then some.

"Easy access," Blanca said when she noticed me eye the booze.

The stage was directly at the back. The proscenium was constructed from mismatched wooden floorboards, polished smooth to remove all bumps and bulges. A heavy curtain the color of emerald stretched across from wing to wing and a series of smaller teaser curtains draped from the rafters. Wooden tables and chairs were carefully arranged in rows facing the stage. Two sets of stairs—two sets of stairs!—curled up on either side of the stage to the second floor balcony. What riches!

"There are seven rooms upstairs, so with you here we're at max capacity. We're pretty sure Old Bunting ran a brothel in the heyday of the Gold Rush," Blanca whispered to us. "Why else would there be all these bedrooms for one man and his wife?"

Blanca led us upstairs and showed us to our sleeping quarters. We were to share a cramped room—dusty blue with a single bed, a vanity, a small wardrobe, and gauzy curtains looking out to the backyard. The room was insufficient for three bodies by most people's standards, but for us, it was downright palatial.

"Dinner's at eight sharp, don't be late. Bette's a real pistol, and she hates tardiness, so best not to start out on the wrong foot. You can meet everyone then. Unpack your things and then do what you want until later. I'm two doors to the left if you need me." Blanca turned and left in a theatrical toss of hair.

We had nothing to unpack save for what little we brought on our trip, which Minny folded neatly into a single shelf in the wardrobe. We ran our fingers over the mirror, the windows, the curtain, the sheets on the bed.

"I'm beat," I said.

The bed was overused and the springs dug into my bony body.

"I'm fired up! I need to get some of this energy out!" Esther began to do jumping jacks in the corner.

"There's a garden in the backyard, and a horse!" Minny said.

In the small yard someone had planted corn, rows of vegetables, and sunflowers. The sunflowers were all dead, or getting there. The corn was stunted to knee-high. The green things, however, were thriving. The horse was a brittle old thing, thin in the knees but still holding a sheen. Its coat was a dappled grey against platinum with a black patch over its right eye. Against the birch tree, the horse's haunches disappeared. We caught each other's eye, the horse staring me down from behind that patch. I slithered behind the curtain and the horse went back to bowing its head to the grass.

"I think those are sweet peas!" Minny said, pointing at a curlicue vine on a trellis.

"Poor thing, all fenced in, that horse needs more space," Esther said.

Beyond the yard loomed trees that blocked the view of the neighbors, if there were any.

We spent our first afternoon at Bette's taking turns sleeping on the bed or playing rounds of pinochle.

"This deck's missing all the aces," Minny said.

"Who needs 'em! We can make our own rules." Esther dealt.

"That's bananas, we need all the cards to play a proper game."

I gave up on the game while Esther arranged the deck in a court marriage scene.

"All the numbered cards are the townsfolk here to see the Page and Knight of Hearts get married."

"You should have the Page of Spades marry the Knight of Hearts, it's always better to join forces, if you extend the family—you extend the army," Minny said.

"Would you two pipe down? It's my turn to sleep." I was still bushed from all the sudden change.

At eight o'clock we made our way downstairs to the dining room, a humble space in the back of the house just through a galley kitchen. I ignored all the pots and pans and appliances. The kitchen was my least favorite room in the house. I was used to hot plates and travel coolers, and those did just fine by me.

"The illustrious Starlings!" Bette welcomed us to the table. "May I introduce you to the Bunting Five: Blanca you know, I'm sure you're already getting along like gangbusters. June, our comedienne; Charlene, our snake charmer and ballerina; Kiki, the violinist; and Franny, our mime. Franny and Blanca have been kind enough to cook our meal tonight."

June was a tiny, symmetrical beauty, a pit bull persona in a body the size of a chihuahua. She used her emery board at the table to file her nails to sharp points. Charlene was a prim and proper sylph, with a hint of an accent like holding her tongue to the roof of her mouth on certain words. Kiki was a voluptuous ingenue, with big teary eyes and a shy, wavering voice. Like Blanca, I couldn't figure out their ages but measured them against myself and the Cuckoo. They weren't young like us but they weren't adults, either. Their skin still defied gravity.

"It's nothing fancy, we had to stretch the pantry with all the new mouths to feed," Blanca said. Franny sat mute and I quickly understood that she never spoke, though out of free will or some disorder, I'd never know. Franny had thick oily hair, and thick oily skin, and eyes the same color as her skin, giving her the effect that she was fading into herself.

"You know, I worked for a while in a kitchen, so I have a few knife skills. I used to work at this bed and breakfast making meat-and-potatoes type stuff. But I'd sneak a garlic clove in the meatballs, or parsley in the steamed carrots, and I think customers got a kick out of it. I like to think I can make simple ingredients trés gourmet."

Blanca scooped us bowls full of shepherd's pie with ground beef and peas and we helped ourselves to a salad made of fresh butter lettuce from the yard. We were used to subsisting on candy or food poached from Maggie: cold buttered noodles and sunflower seeds. Our diet up until now had consisted of sugar, stale foods, and close-to-rotting leftovers.

"That's where Blanca and I met, I was eating at her kitchen and got her fired," Bette said.

"She told the chef she preferred my food and he fired me straightaway."

"He was just jealous because you were more talented."

"So I went with her and turned my ace knife skills into a party trick here at the Bunting house."

"You like the pictures?" Charlene asked, shoving a forkful of mushy peas in my face. She leaned across the table with her tensile and delicate arm. She was stretched tall and thin, towering over the rest of the girls at the table. She had yellow eyes like gashes in her face. Kiki and Franny didn't say a word but concentrated on their shepherd's pies in silence. Occasionally Franny would guffaw at something one of the other girls said and Kiki would smirk or snort.

"Oh yes, very much!"

"Me too. You know, every year when I was a kid I dressed up as the Little Tramp."

"I like Scarlett O'Hara."

"Scarlett O'Hara! What a hag! Now Rhett Butler, there's a character. I like his swagger."

Esther said, "Did you ever see that movie called *The Normandie Cow*? I love that movie. I can really relate to the main girl's friend. She's, like, sexy, but misunderstood." I balked at the bravado of my kid sister, already butting in on other people's conversations with made-up stories. It made me want to choke on my cooked carrot.

"You don't say? Tell us more, Esther," I said.

"Yeah, she grows up with the meanest parents. Her mom and pop don't let her date, stay out late, drink soft drinks, *nothing*."

"Then what?"

"Then what what?"

"Then what happens to the girl?"

"Oh! So, one night she dresses up as a man and sneaks out of the house and goes out on the town. She has a grand old time, flirting with girls, drinking up a storm, dancing, singing. And no one recognizes her! She even gets a little thrill when her teacher walks into the bar where she's singing and doesn't recognize her. So, she does this every night."

"It really is a shame how men get to have all the fun," Charlene said. All the women lifted their glasses and took a swig. "Please, continue, Esther."

"So, anyway, this girl, I can't remember her name, she does this every night for, like, a week or something, and there's like this weird sub-story with the crush on her teacher, which is gross and such a scandal, and her parents find out but they're so impressed by her talent that they just let it go... To be honest I don't really remember the ending."

"I suppose she and the teacher get together happily ever after? And now that she has a man her parents finally let her out of the house?" June had pushed her food aside and was back to her emery board.

"I remember now!" Now Minny was in on the game. "The girl figures out how much she loves performing and goes on to become this huge Hollywood star and bamboozles all these big wigs. It's one of those ambiguous endings, ya know?"

"Yeah that's it! Pearl, do you remember that one?" When she spoke, Esther spit a piece of potato onto her plate and plopped it back in her mouth.

Disgusting.

"Sounds like a familiar story." I could no longer tell which was which: the rouge or the flush of Esther's performance.

"The pictures are for the plebeian. Entertainment is all about dance and music," June said.

"Entertainment of all sorts is valued in this house," Bette said. "So Starlings, what is it you can do?"

"Do? We're fifteen."

"Yes, but there must be something you can do, something you can offer. Juggling? Underwater breathing?"

"We can contort!" Minny said. I'd never heard that word before and felt my body tense at the idea of performing an unknown definition. Our unscripted tumbling in the desert could hardly qualify as a marketable skill.

"Contortionists! You don't say? Now there's a skill we haven't seen yet at the revue."

Charlene began to clear the table. "You know, when I was little I used to run up to the sand dune near our house looking for snakes. Oh how I loved snakes—garter, moccasin, rattle. Once I had the nerve to squeeze into their holes. The walls of the burrow were lined with snake skins—the scales glittered and twinkled like precious stones. At the pit, the owner of the burrow had arranged the skulls of its kill like a small shrine. I wasn't afraid, though. That's when I heard the dinner bell and knew it was time to run home. When I emerged, I was stretched out, as you see me now in the flesh. And here I am, taller, and thinner, and older. That's a sort of contortion, no?"

"I think that's enough chatter for tonight, let's clean up and settle down." Bette left her plate on the table for the rest of us to clear. "Time for me to retire. See you in the AM, girls."

The girls poured drinking chocolate in mugs. Charlene, Blanca, and June snuck whisky in their drinks, and shook the bottle at us.

"Want a plug?" Blanca asked.

Esther poured a capful into her chocolate.

"Esther!" I punched my baby sister in the arm. We were supposed to be on our best behavior, we were guests. Guests that needed to stay.

"What? I'm settling down, like Bette told us to," she said.

"Can you hang?" June asked Minny and me.

Minny scoffed and drank straight from the bottle, twisting her face in a way that put the rest of the girls in stitches.

I poured a bit of the stuff in my chocolate and took tiny sips, careful not to drink too much.

We fell asleep one on top of the other on our crickety bed and woke with creases on our cheeks from all the contact. Bette loomed over us with an armful of fresh towels.

"Get up," she said. "Time to go shopping. If you're gonna join our little family, you'll need new everything."

WOLVES MASQUERADING AS WOOLENS

"One of my many talents is styling and tailoring," Charlene said. She had been recruited by Bette to accompany us to the consignment shop for new clothes.

"I want in too," Blanca said. "I could use a new bathing suit for the end of summer."

At the shop Charlene found a pair of rabbit fur gloves buried in a nickel clothing bin.

"Live like a bourgeois, but dress like a demigod, yes?" She said. We were all jealous of the find and ravaged through the bins likes starving wolves.

I chose a silk swing skirt in sea-foam green and a cream blouse with a clara collar. Charlene pinned the top with a lucite brooch in the shape of a scarab. Esther found an asymmetrical dress in the latest fashion—not my style—in some new fabric that stretched over her body and felt like rose petals to the touch.

"*Zut alors*!" Charlene was holding a scandalous two-piece bathing suit, yellow with itty-bitty white dots, that tied in a knot at the bosom. "Here's a suit for you, Blanca dear."

"I would never!" Blanca said. She winked at me and grabbed the suit, stuffing it in her basket, underneath an orange A-line shirt and blouse set with big tortoiseshell buttons.

Minny emerged from the dressing room wearing a glossy purple tuxedo so oversized on her tiny frame that she looked like a deflated whoopee cushion. The suit was, admittedly, a find—it was adorned with a thick velvet stripe that ran down the leg, a matching double-breasted coat with gold Irish knot buttons, and a matching cummerbund.

"You can fix this, right Charlene?" Minny was trying to see the back of herself in the mirror.

"June's not going to be too happy if you choose a suit—she's the cross-dresser on the bill." I was fiddling with half-empty perfume bottles for a new scent.

"Cross-dressing is archaic, anyhow. What's one more woman wearing a Le Smoking? But—you're gonna have to show more skin if you want the tips. And you're going to want the tips if you want to stick around. Bette will want to see that you can make her some money. I love it, though the cummerbund may be a bit over the top." Charlene was pinching and prodding the fabric around Minny's shoulders to mold them into form-fitting peaks.

"I like the cummerbund, it makes me stand up straight," Minny said, sucking in her gut, sticking out her chest, and admiring her figure in the mirror.

"All right, but I'm not coming to your rescue when June sees you're mooching her act. Though she could use a little humility, if you ask me. That girl never learned to share, I swear," Blanca said.

"Darling, you look the right amount of handsome. Screw June, this suit suits you."

Charlene was now eyeballing a deep mahogany gauze number with undulating layers of thin fabric.

"Don't you think this will be great for the Faun? We can add some variety to our costuming. This looks just like Nijinsky's nymphs in the Paris premiere at the Theatre de Champs-Élysées. It's a bit antiquated, but that seems fitting for my faun, no?"

She paired the dress with a set of demure velvet slippers with a kitten heel in a color the shopgirl called "Moonless Sky."

"You really think Bette is going to ask us to join the revue?" Minny asked.

"Seems to me she's set on it. You're a triple threat, a guaranteed boost to her bottom line. Pretty triplets who can perform? Who wouldn't eat that up." Charlene pretended to gnaw on Esther's arm and Esther squealed and bit her back.

"Speaking of eating, we have a few bucks left, what do you say we get some burgers?"

"Burgers? Really, Blanca? We're supposed to be watching our figures."

"One beef patty isn't going to hurt. Besides, we can make it up with cottage cheese salad for dinner."

Charlene ironed her flat stomach with her hands and grinned.

"Fine, but let's get some beer, too."

The only "grown up" restaurant in town was a bar and burger joint, according to Kiki. It was about three in the afternoon but since we had skipped lunch to shop we were famished. Blanca ordered us pitchers of beer and five burgers with fries. Esther gushed over the jukebox, playing songs from her favorite over-the-top musical. She came back for a second serving of beer and I caught her hand.

"Gluttony is a nasty habit for a young girl," I said.

"Who made you boss?" She grabbed the pitcher and poured herself another, sloshing the amber liquid down her arm and all over the table, not bothering to sop it up. I held a soggy french fry to my face and threw it at her, missing the mark by a long shot.

"Would you rather date a famous dancer or musician?" Blanca asked.

"Dancer," Minny said. "Then he'd have all those moves." Which she demonstrated with a rotation of her hips.

"Maybe you two could do a duet in your dreams," I said, snatching her beer away and taking a swig. The cool bubbles melted the tight coil of my insides.

The pub had a small television behind the bar. The ancient bartender (Blanca called him Father Time) leaned against the drink rail eating chips and watching a TV western starring this year's hottest male lead, Jean-Paul Devereux.

"I wish Bette would let us get a television. It'd be great for research!" Blanca said.

"Bette will never go for it, she thinks it's nothing but a distraction. And I agree—time spent in front of the screen should be time spent practicing. Why watch other people do things when we could be doing them ourselves?" Charlene fiddled the fries on her plate.

"You think Jean-Paul is a homosexual?" Esther asked. She didn't even bother to lower her voice.

"God, I hope so, I love a good scandal." Charlene motioned for the bill. Blanca motioned for a refill.

"Well, he probably needs someone more feminine as a stand-in for his social events," I said.

"You'd do that? Sacrifice love for money?" Esther asked.

"Sure, why not? And it's not just about money. It's about exposure. Think of all the cameras on me! Besides, we could both have lovers on the side."

"That sounds awful."

"I'm into it," said Blanca. "Why don't you dial him up? For a fake date call: 555 555 5555."

"No, thank you. I'll wait for my Prince Charming to swoop me up in his fancy car, all the way to Paris." Esther had drunk one too many and was slurring her words. She leaned her body against mine and I let her put her arm around my shoulder.

"I didn't know cars could cross the Atlantic." She shot me a murderous look.

"Bottoms up, we have to scram if we're going to make it to dinner on time," Blanca said.

We all shoved down the last bits of fries and burgers or sips of beers, wiped the juices on our new skirts, and ran out the door without paying.

"Save this for later," Charlene laughed, pocketing the leftover shopping money.

We showed up just in time for the dinner June and Kiki had prepared, a predictable slab of steak with green beans almondine.

"What, no appetite?" June asked as we pushed our food around our plates. "Or is my cooking just that bad?"

"You smell like booze," Kiki said, sniffing at Minny's shoulder.

"Where's Bette?" Minny asked. "I want to show her our new togs."

"Never mind where Bette is," June said. "And if you're not going to eat, you can clean and clear." She shoved her plate away, took Kiki and Franny's out from under their forks, and then pushed the plates toward my sisters. "Bette says you're going to be staying a while so you'll have to start in on the chores. Starting tonight. And we're skipping tea. Goodnight, girls."

Minny and Esther were too drunk to wash the dishes properly so I took the lead while they sang some new song they'd picked up and performed a tango across the linoleum.

"You dry and you put away, I'll do the sudsing."

"Can you believe it, June said Bette said we'll be staying!"

"But we've never performed!"

"She don't have to know that. Besides, we've performed plenty of times for each other."

"Doesn't." Minny corrected. "Doesn't have to know that."

"You know Minny, you looked like Bette in that suit today." Esther was playing with a towel as a turban on her head.

"Nonsense! Bette is an Amazon queen compared to me."

"I think June looks like that painting from the trailer, that pinkish hairless woman with those rosy cheeks."

"I think she looks like a possum," I said, flinging soap at my sisters. They shoved me out of the way with their hips and dove into the murky soaped-up water. They were careless with their washing. Esther scrubbed the glasses at high speed and Minny barely dabbed the sopping silver with her towel. Their hands sloshed water all over the wooden countertop. I cringed at this slipshod routine but my own hands were stinging from hot water and bleach so I kept mum.

"All done, first one upstairs gets the center of the bed!" Esther said, not bothering to drain the sink.

We darted up the stairs and grabbed at each other's nightgown hems for first in line. Esther and Minny vied for the top but Minny tripped Esther who tumbled sideways, face flat on the wallpaper. I stepped over her and shoved Minny on the last step to the floor.

"Ow, Pearl. That was too hard. You made me skin my knee."

"You know what they say: you snooze, you lose the best place to snooze."

Once upstairs I stationed myself in the middle of the bed. Minny and Esther were panting, pretending to be out of breath for the fun of it. Minny, if you ask me, was rubbing her knee far too dramatically.

"Where do you think Bette went?" I sat up to

make way for my sisters.

"Mexico."

"The Moon."

"Jean-Paul Devereux's mansion."

"The moon over Jean-Paul Devereux's mansion in Mexico?"

"I'm serious, we just got here, why would she leave?"

"She probably had a trip planned. Don't overthink it, Pearl. We got a place to stay. If the lady of the house wants to skedaddle, that's her choice." Minny had stopped soothing her skinned knee and was now yawning into her arm. Esther was picking her nails and fighting off her heavy eyelids.

I woke in sweats from visions of our old mare and the trailer. I dreamt that my own arms were choking me and that I needed to cut them off or I would suffocate. I woke to see if the dappled horse was still there but when I went to the window, it was gone.

In my half-sleep I felt my way through the room looking for the toilet. But the bathroom was not where I remembered it was, and, in fact, even the feeling of my feet coming off the bed was puzzling. When I woke I was supposed to be in a single-room home, the kitchen, living quarters, and bedroom all in one space. The bathroom was through a half-door with an inlaid handle grip. The shower and the toilet were on top of one another—sometimes I peed in the shower so that my urine could wash down the drain alongside soap and shampoo in one efficient stream.

But this morning there was no inlaid handle grip, and I could not find a familiar wall. When I reached the window overlooking the yard dying in the dry spell, I remembered where I was: a theater in Sky-on-the-Lake, in a home full of strangers I had to win over. The platinum horse slept standing up under a small tree. His coat reflected the fading moonlight in my eyes, allowing me to see my two sisters. They were still asleep, their legs warped around one another so as to appear not like legs at all, but like the globby sculptures of a volcano we made for the last science fair.

I made my way down the hall to find the toilet (I always had such a full bladder at night) and saw a light peering out from under the door of Bette's office. The rest of the hall was dark. Every night for a week I made this trek from my bedroom to the bathroom, always with the light from under Bet-te's door, always with the same uncanny feeling of the newcomer in a worn-in place. By the end of the week, I woke and knew not to look for the handle, the kitchen, or the living quarters. I knew to run my hand on the wallpaper until I found the doorknob to the hall, four doors down to the bathroom on the right. And then, relief.

While Blanca and Charlene welcomed us into their home, seeing us as their pets and playthings, and Kiki was too introspective to project any obvi-ous hostility, our arrival made June's and Franny's blood boil. Franny was always a bit anxious about her position in the crew—mimes were well out of style, and with the tenuous financial situation of a live show, everyone knew they risked the boot in order to make room for more profitable performers. But Franny's dismay manifested as retreat and the cold shoulder. To June, we represented her bygone youth. She was the oldest of the crew, and thus the most likely to get kicked from the show. She was a cross-dressing comedian with flimsy routines.

Her go-to was a set she called Salt N' Vinegar, in which she played both sides of a duo, a schizophrenic routine between a wise-guy suit and a ditzy blonde. There was something more to her misgivings, however. I watched her as she clung to Bette at the dinner table that first night. She kept one eye on Bette the entire time and leaned in to listen to any conversation Bette began with any of the other girls.

I found out from Blanca that Bette had gone south for some undisclosed business finagling. Bette left about once a month or so to drum up new opportunities, scout for venues, and she always returned with exotic gifts. She left June in charge while she went off on these voyages, a prospect that made me stiffen in my chair.

"You're on dishes again tonight, Starlings. And try not to be so filthy! You're leaving standing water around the sink, wet towels that need hanging dripping all over our rugs to gather mold and god knows what else," June said after our Friday night meal. She'd been shirking all the chores onto us.

"Give them a break, June, they're only fifteen. You remember what it was like to be fifteen, dontcha?" Charlene put an arm around Esther's shoulder, pinching her cheek.

"We've been on cleaning duty for a week straight now, it's not fair," Esther said.

"She's just bitter. She's been losing laughs for some time now," Charlene said.

"I'd say your perverse obsession with *the Faun* is getting a little stale too, Charley." June was sitting at the table filing her nails, using the emery board like a machete. Charlene and Franny were paired together for an upcoming show—Charlene was all leg and Franny was all head. They had been practicing a rendition of *Afternoon of the Faun*. Charlene was a gifted dancer, but very predictable. Franny, on the other hand, wasn't much of a mover but she was a magnetic performer. Charlene wore a chain of ivy around her flesh-toned slinky bodysuit, heavy black eye makeup that curled up to her brows, and two twisted horns attached to a laurel wreath around her head. Franny dressed as the veil—wearing a sheath of white gauze. Charlene danced around Franny, clomping her heels to evoke the sound of hooves. Franny responded to Charlene's movements with improvised drawings that she first showed to the audience then laid on the floor as a path for Charlene to follow. She pranced on the paper trail toward her death, collapsing on Franny in blissful reverie.

I giggled at the image of June reaching for a memory from age fifteen—a bathing suit at a summer lake, a dipped ice cream cone, a first kiss, the straps of a favorite jumper—but finding nothing but the image of a wrinkling grape in her mind.

"What's so funny, Pearl?"

I stifled my laugh in my napkin and began to clear.

"You girls better start thinking about your act, we can't be giving handouts to freeloaders forever. When Bette gets back, she's going to want to see some sort of audition."

"Come on girls, I'll help with the dishes," Blanca said, leading us to the kitchen.

"She's gonna rip our scalps off!" Esther said.

"And that Franny, I think she's trying to make us fat with all that coconut cake. She keeps sneaking us more at tea!" Minny said, rubbing her flat belly.

"They're harmless," Blanca said. "But June's right about one thing, Bette's gonna want to see some sort of work from you three, if you're going to stick around. You say you can contort?"

"Yeah, we've been doing it for years now, right sis?" Minny said.

"Oh sure! We have this one act we call the Human Celtic Knot. We lay down and wrap our legs and arms around the other's legs and arms and around the other's legs and arms and bada-bing, we made an unbreakable loop of limbs!" Esther took Minny's cue to ham it up.

Blanca laughed and shook her locks.

"All right, if you say so. But a word of advice: get to practicing."

"Let's do the small box trick!" Esther said. We were up late discussing our plans in bed. "I read about it in one of the Cuckoo's dailies. Apparently, in Romania, six-foot-tall men squeeze themselves inside a container no larger than a women's size five shoe box! We can make it a magic act. Picture it: three boxes on stage with glass fronts facing the audience. Inside Box Number One is a dove. Box Number Two contains a rabbit. And Box Number Three is a bouquet of roses."

"Roses? Does it have to be roses?"

"Fine, dandelions, daffodils, whatever you want, Minny dear. Inside Box Number Three is a bouquet of dandelions. We'll get Blanca to drop little velvet curtains over the front and Kiki to distract the audience with a song."

"What about, 'Dream a Little Dream of Me?'" I asked.

"Pearl, you're so outdated," Esther said. "So we three climb in the boxes. Then, Blanca unfurls the curtains and voilà! There we are inside the box-es, like little presents! Now, who wants to be the bunny?"

I fell asleep dreaming of acrobatic jackrabbits and synchronized swimming hares. I woke in the morning to find Minny had delivered three hat boxes pilfered from the attic.

"We should all be wearing the hats that were in these boxes. Once we're out, we take our curtsy, and tip our hats, and inside the hat will be the dove, the rabbit, and the flowers! Isn't that clever?"

We practiced the trick all morning, skipping breakfast and lunch. By mid afternoon I had dislocated my hip, at which point we decided it was time for a break. We paused for dinner, a stilted conversation over June's (dry) chuck roast and (soggy) pearl onions. We had vowed to return to practice after dinner but after just closing our eyes, we fell asleep at the foot of our bed.

First thing next morning, we returned to our hat boxes.

"Let's try a new angle," Minny said, getting stuck for two hours before we managed to pry her out with a concoction of butter, baby powder, and three of Charlene's hairpins.

"I have an idea," Esther said. She was covered in animal fat and talc. She looked like the bottom of a cake pan. "If this stuff can get a body out, it can also get a body in, you see what I mean? The head is the least flexible bit, but once that's tucked away, the rest is easy! You dive in headfirst, then bend your legs backward over your head, and around the torso, like so." Esther demonstrated her tactic in swift movements, and sure enough, all of her was inside the hatbox. She had laid her chest and face down like a roughhousing dog and folded her upturned legs to rest beside her torso. Minny cheered and placed a straw bucket hat with a plume of white feathers atop our sister's head.

"How'd you figure that out?" I was dumbfounded by my baby sister's ingenuity.

"Be happy, Pearly, we got ourselves an act. You look like you're gonna blow a fuse!"

After a few more excruciating hours of practice, we had the trick down.

"We can call it One Thousand and One Coattails," Minny said. "Esther you stay curled up as the genie in the box and me and Pearl will play Princess and the Shah. Pearl, you play the Shah."

Minny draped her arm dramatically across her eyes.

"Oh, woe is me, woe is me! A princess without a prince. And a stepmother who is cruel and stepsisters who are even more cruel. My only friends are mice and barnyard animals. If only someone would come to my rescue and save me from this cursed castle. If only I could remember those magic words that witch in the woods told me to recite if I ever things got real bad. What were those words?"

"Fee fi hum hum," Esther muffled from her box.

"Fee fi hum hum! That's it! Fee fi hum hum! Fee fi hum hum!"

Esther popped out of the box like a spring, twirling in pirouettes, and landed at my feet. She crossed her arms and spread her legs wide.

"You rang?"

"Why do I always have to play the villain?"

"Because, Pearl, you play it so well."

Bette returned from her trip that Sunday. She'd only been gone a week but Blanca insisted we make a cake and celebrate her arrival with champagne. She baked a towering monstrosity with thirteen layers of white sponge and thirteen layers of white buttercream and pink marzipan rosettes. She scrawled "Welcome Back Bette" in blue icing at the top and placed three taper candles next to each line.

"What? For me? Girls, you shouldn't have." Bette looked worn down and sun-soaked. Her skin a bit more deserted, taut, stretched too tightly and closely against her bones and muscle. She promptly propped her feet up on a spare seat at the table and grabbed a slice of cake.

"This is delightful. Kiki, you've outdone yourself!"

"It has marzipan, your favorite."

"You always satiate my sweet tooth, to be sure. I brought something for you all, too." Bette reached in her pockets and produced a handful of turquoise. "I brought back some serape blankets from Pea Shrub Canyon, too. Try to incorporate the goods into the act somehow. You can make up some sort of cowboy and Indian skit, or reenact the Alamo. Now, what have my girls been up to while I was away?"

"The Starlings have been up to quite a lot. They got something to show you, don't you Starlings?" June was serving herself another slice of cake, straight from the center. It was true, the cake was tasty. The zing of lemon danced with a gingerly hint of vanilla and the bites disappeared on the tip of my tongue before coating my insides with a thin layer of all the things good girls are made of—sugar, a flirtatious amount of spice, and, you know, the niceties. Maybe this cake was my one-way ticket from rotten egg to good-humored gal. I motioned for another slice by wiggling my plate at Blanca.

"Is that so? What do you have to show me, Starlings?"

"We're aiming to join your revue this fall, Ms. Bunting," Esther was playing her best innocent ingenue.

"We've been practicing a new trick like you've never seen," Minny linked Esther's arm.

Bette glanced at me, waiting for my two cents, but I ate my cake in diminutive bites, scraping the frosting off first with the back of my fork and licking the sugary spread with the tip of my tongue. Charlene grabbed at her cake with her hands. These girls had no manners. They said, did, and ate whatever they wanted, however they wanted, whenever the mood struck them. The Cuckoo had her faults but she at least had taught us some humility.

The girls were passing around champagne, swigging from the bottle. When it came to me, I drank a long slug of the syrupy fizz and let the bubbles pop my eyes out of my skull. I poured myself a glass, drank that to the bottom, and then poured myself another. No one could judge me from their high horses.

"Well all right then, let's see what you can do," Bette took her feet off the chair and drank my second glass of champagne.

Esther set up the three hat boxes in the center receiving hall. She beckoned everyone with a booming announcement.

"Come on in and see the most mind-boggling, mind-blowing, jaw-dropping magical contortionist trick this side of the Rockies. It's one of a kind, or I should say three of a kind, starring the stupendous Starling Sisters."

"That's not part of the trick," I whispered to Minny.

"She's off book!"

"You should have had more of that champagne."

"I think you had enough for the both of us, Pearly."

Blanca stepped up to reveal the contents of the boxes: the rabbit, the dove, and the flowers. She then replaced the tops and drew a curtain to shield our maneuvering from our audience. She distracted them with a quick little knife trick and sing-a-along—*well, Mama, she didn't 'low me just to stay out all night long, Oh Lord*— and then theatrically removed the curtain.

One-two-three we popped out of the hat boxes, Minny, Esther, and me, a curtsy, a bow, and a hat-tip. This was followed by the sound of several hands clapping and Charlene's whistles.

"My, my, that was quite a show." Bette was clapping, too, but held her hands to her face to mask a yawn. "Now where'd you get such a penchant for performance at your young age?"

I wanted to tell her about the Cuckoo, about the restraint we practiced in the trailer, that the act sprung from necessity and not sheer will or imagination.

"I think they'd make a super addition to our act, Bette. We could use some fresh faces," Blanca said.

Esther piped up. "Just think of the bill: the Starling Sisters, famous triplet beauties with voices like songbirds and bodies like rubber, not one, not two, but three tensile treats to wrap your eyes around."

"Well, aren't you the little businesswoman? All right, we'll give it a try. You'll debut at the Halloween show."

We went to bed singing, "*Well, my mama didn't love me, didn't love me, didn't love me. My mama didn't love me, didn't love me like she loves a high flyin' man.*"

LAST NIGHT THEY LOVED YOU

The Halloween show was the revue's most lucrative event of the year. Each year the Bunting girls put on a dinner party murder mystery: Bette and her brood, doomed party of six. It was also the only show at the Bunting house in which Bette appeared on stage. She played the dupe, killed at the start in some brutal way (seventeen knife stabbings, chloroform followed by brain removal, throat slit by a violin bow). The other women would do their skits and then die off one by one until everyone met their maker, and it was revealed that Bette had been alive all along as the murderer. They'd then perform in a torturous living-dead tête-à-tête. I was buckling under the pressure of entering the show at the height of its popularity. I struggled to get the routine down, bumbling and bumping into my sisters, my voice coming out as squeaks and burbles.

This year, however, the Halloween show had a Shakespearean theme. June decided we should play the three court jesters. Charlene sewed our costumes in alternating colors: red and white for me, white and black for Minny, and red and black for Esther.

When we twirled and wrapped and swiveled around one another, the costumes became a hypnotic device. The effect was dizzying if we rotated our bodies fast enough like helicopter blades.

The night before the show Bette kept us after dinner for a pep talk.

"You know the deal. I want quality, fashionable work, not just slapstick gags and easy jokes. And absolutely no minstrels, no blackface. Unless it's crucial to the narrative, of course. Other than that, it's free game up there. I know your routines, but surprise me. I want something fresh this time."

The lineup went like this: Charlene would open as the snake charmer with the slithering body, Kiki would do a burlesque to a solo violin caprice, Franny would mime a swan song, June and Blanca were to follow with their comedy bit, we were to make our debut with our hatbox routine, and then we would all finish with our ensemble extravaganza. Bette wrote our grand finale for the night. She called it "Much Ado about Everything." We were dressed as lords and earls, or gentlemen of various elite lineages. We wore breeches and codpieces, and pointed shoes that killed my feet. I was used to performing barefoot, but I much preferred dressing in men's clothes—there was such agility in a pair of pants! The authority of a button-up and cufflinks was intoxicating.

Kiki would lead us in a felice violin ditty as we pantomimed a poker scene.

We began the act talking politics:

Neither candidate is very good... The lesser of

two evils... I don't care for either of them, to be honest ... So-and-so would be a disaster... A danger... A joke...

"Did you see Hero at the ball last night?"

"*Quel scandale!*"

"A mockery to the Prince!"

"Why, because she dressed as a hound?"

"I could barely keep my paws off her."

"Bite thy tongue, here is my Bitch."

"And your Beatrice, your queen?"

"This hand you've dealt is chilling as your precious Queen."

"I'd gladly offer my hand to warm her up."

And so on with these bon mots until June's character offends Charlene's, leading to a brawl. We all get in the fray and strangle one another to death. Kiki leads us out with more violin, swiping the poker chips into her instrument case.

My sisters were backstage fidgeting and rehashing our routine while I laid on my stomach to watch June and Blanca's routine from underneath the curtain. I figured it would be good research if I took notes on Blanca's skill for wordplay. They were dressed in drag as Gentlemen Gangsters. Blanca dreamed up the idea. She was always coming up with bananas skits that, for some reason, Bette would sign off on. The gist was that they were these two well-mannered but hapless British thugs who spoke in puns and double entendres.

June played the straight man, Mauricio, and Blanca played Arthur, the clueless goofball. They wore matching bowler hats—Mauricio's too small, and Arthur's too big—and matching pin stripe suits, both in comically large sizes.

Blanca walked on stage. She looked around at the rafters, oblivious to her surroundings.

"What a day! What a day! The first sunny afternoon in London in, oh, I'd say ten years. Yessir, what a day. I better enjoy my time outside while I can. No sir, this weather surely will not last." She sat down and cracked a bottle of beer. She took her time tasting and swallowing, relishing the flavor. June entered as Mauricio. She stomped on the floorboards to maximize her diminutive physicality. Blanca gave a sheepish look and stopped drinking mid-sip.

"Arthur? What are you doing on this side of town?"

"Mauricio! Fine day, huh? Fine day for a walk in the park, that's what I thought to myself."

"Yes, fine day, just fine."

"And you? What brings you to Spitalfields?"

"Business. I have a bone to pick with the butcher." June took out her switchblade and began to pick under nails.

"Ho ho! A bone with the butcher! That's too rich, too rich."

"He owes me money. A lot of it. He won't be rich after I've gotten hold of his pockets, let me tell you."

"Oh Maury, you always crack me up. You know, for such a scary-looking guy you have an excellent sense of humor."

"What do you mean? Scary-looking?" Itty bitty June puffed her chest and stood on her tiptoes to loom over Blanca. Blanca took a nervous and audible gulp of beer.

"Oh, I meant it in the best of ways! It's good to be scary in our business, don't you agree? I'm at quite the disadvantage, no one ever takes me seriously. Then again, I do have the art of deception on my side. You're good at your job, is what I meant to say."

"Why, thank you, Arthur."

The voices on stage became familiar to me—of course, these were the two swans in the boxes from the show in the desert. Though I knew it, I felt a tinge of disappointment at the parroting—the repetition pointed to a lack of imagination. But there was also a freedom in settling into another persona that could loop in and out of performances. Who would I be in that box? Did I have any control? I decided I would close my eyes and surrender, and allow the character to emerge.

"Say, Mauricio, this wouldn't be Paul McShannonhan the butcher would it?

"One and the same. Why do you ask?"

"I have a beef with him myself. That's the real reason I came down here."

"Looks to me like you had another agenda." June sized Blanca's beer up.

"Oh, a mere pitstop! Besides, one must do what one must to get a little boost of confidence." She offered a sip to June, who waved it away with her hand.

"What's your beef with the butcher?"

"You know when I was on the lamb? McShan-nonhan hit on my little lady, the old cow. If you like, we can go together, I'll be your wingman!"

"No, no I prefer to do it a loin."

"Very well. I suppose too much activity might attract the pigs anyhow."

"So, Paulie hit on your old lady, eh? Bet that hit a tender spot."

"Please! Spare me. I could give a damn really. I just crave a good old-fashioned ribbing after my time on the run. I'm a wise guy through and through, you know."

"Well, shucks, you've got guts, I'll give you that. Let's go together! We can flank attack him!"

"Oh goody! You know, Mauricio, there really is more to you than meats the eye."

"Oh go on, I'm turning red."

At that, June and Blanca turned away from the audience, picked up two machetes, and with an exaggerated tip-toe, sauntered off from opposite sides of the stage. The lights on the stage dimmed and spotlit the backstage, revealing the silhouette of the two gangsters and another figure, Paulie McShannonhan the butcher (played by Kiki), who held a meat cleaver in mid-chop. Franny, who in her refusal to speak harnessed a real predilection for sound effects, was on the mic making chopping, mooing, crunching, squishing, and humming sounds, as the butcher sang along to his task. Blanca and June flanked Paulie (Kiki), raised their weapons, and Franny screamed into the mic. Lights out. The audience stood and gave an ovation, laughing, wiping tears from their eyes, or collapsed in heaps on their chairs. I was backstage mentally taking note of every nuance.

"Okay Starlings, you're up," June said, glowing from her knock-out performance.

Blanca was out front distracting the audience with her knife and flame routine while Charlene set up our boxes behind the curtain. From backstage I heard the gasps and delight of an audience facing flames. We curled inside in our method: head first, feet last. My shoulders were stooped, pitched forward, and I gently vibrated them back then forward, twice in a downward shrug, like a child pretending to gallop horses. I held my breath, waiting for the signal from Blanca to burst forth, a tap on top of my container. I was beginning to lose my breath, the stale unmoving air sticking to my nose hairs. My throat was coated in must and my tongue was weighty and strange. I felt something flutter on my shoulder and tried to flick it away without moving the sides of the box. In the dark I saw two pin-head-sized eyes, green, resting on my arm. A moth. *So that's what's been eating at all our sweaters*, I thought. I was forgetting to breathe so I made shapes of what I thought were words with my mouth but made sure no noise came through the gaps of my lips, nor behind my teeth. During this epochal silence, I experienced the sensation of hearing grief and hearing memory. I could hear what must have been speech—humming, gagging, drooling, roaring, hissing, rushing, zapping, buzzing, floating outside the box. I could hear my sisters' breathing through vibrations from the floorboards. The noises translated into honeycomb patterns behind my eyes that I could read like album notes.

And a one and a two and a one, two, three, go! The performance was lost to me. Perhaps because we had practiced the skit so much it felt like habit, a rerun, the moves were alive in my muscles and not my mind. One moment I was coiled in my hatbox along with a wriggling dove, and the next I was linked arm-in arm with my sisters, confronted with an encore and an ovation. Bette pushed us all to reappear on stage. I felt my sisters' hands in mine but was blinded by light and noise. I could see nothing but small twinkling lights in my line of vision. I heard the sound of hands flapping against one another. Fingers in mouths making whistles. I listened for my name but heard only *oooooooooooo*.

"Give 'em some more," I heard Bette stage-whisper.

So we sang the only song we all knew by heart.

> *Up above the world so high,*
> *like a diamond ...*

In the course of a night, we were no longer scraggly girls with limited control of our bodies. We were budding women who had mastered our gangling appendages, cordoned into a routine rife with tapered waists and feats of contortion that sent our audience into a tailspin.

"Do you feel her pain, or her pain, when they've stubbed a toe?" Charlene asked us that night over a late snack.

"Yeah, Pearl, can you see what Esther and Minny are seeing, even if you aren't in the room?"

"If you can, we should market you as a magic trick."

"Or bring you to the horse races."

"Oh sure, we can read each other's minds, finish each other's—"

"Sentences."

How did Minny and Esther become so close? Where was I? I only felt a distance, a denial of the attractive force of a blood line. I didn't understand star systems, I was on my own planet.

IN THESE GOLDEN YEARS

"I invest my money in you, and you invest your time in making the best show possible, deal?"

After our successful Halloween debut, Bette speculated that we would bring her fame and fortune at last. She bought us more dresses, shoes, and two more beds so we no longer had to share. We arranged them like bunk beds to leave us space to move around, space to keep us limber. She paid for haircuts in the new cropped-and-wave.

She took the time to teach us how to apply rouge (Evening in Paris) so that our cheekbones contoured like two fat almonds, eyeliner (Midnight at the Moroccan) so that our eyes popped *zing*, and lipstick (Havana Sunrise) so that when we sang, the words appeared as though they were dancing off our lips. She let us read her magazines and play at her vanity so we could learn to be real women.

Think glamour is only for Hollywood starlets? Think you need a contract with RKO to feel like you deserve beauty? Think again! There's no need to let your natural beauty go to waste just because you're stuck at home with the kids or sitting at a typewriter in an office. Besides, your husband (and your boss) will love the new gorgeous you!

Subscribe now to The Glamorous Woman *and discover your most beautiful self. Winter, Spring, Summer, or Fall, we have all the best seasonal tips. Take our* What Type Are You? Quiz *to receive custom advice for your face shape, body type, hair color, eyes, nose, lips, and hips! Don't worry, there's no studying required! Not sure if you are a bombshell blonde or a hip waif? Girly-girl or outdoorsy-obsessed? Swanlike sophisticate or enticing exotic? Take the quiz and subscribe to* The Glamorous Woman *to reveal the secrets to looking (and feeling!) your very best.*

We'll show you how to achieve the most graceful neckline, perfect the pin curl, and how to restore beauty lost to time (and all that stress from running a household!) Whether you should go for the latest bob, bubble cut, poodle cut, bouffant, pageboy or pixie. How to apply perfume. Facial expressions to practice in the mirror for delaying wrinkles. And more!

In the bonus Glamorous Woman Charm and Etiquette Guide, *we provide you with answers from the experts to those pesky social questions: Got a Hot Date with the Mister? Meeting His Mother for the First Time? Corporate Cocktail Party Coming Up? We'll give you the best advice for clothes, makeup, and hairstyles, and icebreaker suggestions to boot. With this guide, you're sure to be the hit of any party.*

If you subscribe now, we'll even throw in a suggested diet plan from licensed doctors to keep you fit and trim, to assure you won't add any extra padding to your lovely figure.

The war is over ladies! No need to ration your beauty. Your country calls you to arms so powder your noses, apply that Patriot Red lipstick, and order now!

I felt like the swan in *The Ugly Duckling*, though I knew we'd always be ducks no matter how much powder we applied to our faces. We were playing with Bette's collection of compact cases and I barely recognized myself in the tiny shell-shaped mirror. I looked to my sisters to match me, but I could no longer discern their identities, nor did they match what I was seeing in my reflection. Minny was admiring herself in a martini glass-shaped multi-colored eye compact. The stem of the glass was a mascara wand. She applied the device to her lashes and *pop pop*! Her eyes mushroomed to hula-hoop proportions. Esther was playing with a demure all-in-one, a burgundy Max Factor lined with gold.

"Hold on girls, I want to use a new color on you but I left the bag in my car."

Once it was safe to assume Bette was out of earshot, I asked my sisters where they thought Bette really went off to all the time. There could only be so many trips for serapes and stones.

"I bet she's been carrying on a long-distance affair with a major executive at an up-and-coming movie studio. He's going to leave his wife and children and marry her. He's the only man she ever loved and ever will." Esther was applying fake lashes to

Minny.

"Where do you come up with this stuff?" June was standing in the doorway, her arms extended against the frame like she was holding the building up with her own bicepular strength. "Does Bette know you're in here?"

"She said we can practice our makeup."

"I doubt she'd want your filthy fingers in her good foundation. I've seen your hygienic habits— they're slim to none." She grabbed a powder puff from Esther's hand and stuffed it back in its pink box. "You can apply as much lipstick or rouge or what-have-you as you want, you can try to make yourself pretty in the traditional sense, but if you don't have a routine down, what's the point? A person can only look at a face for so long. You're good, but you're not *that* good. Your audiences are still slim. Quit your lollygagging in Bette's stuff and get to practicing. You may still be kids but this isn't pretend anymore. This is real life. This is how we make our living."

"Cool it June, I know they're here." Bette was back and waving a lipstick wand (Princess Pink) under June's nose. June grabbed the lipstick and walked away. Three tongues stuck out at June's back.

"Why is she such a sourpuss?"

"Yeah, what does she have against us?"

"Don't mind her. She has mommy issues. She's afraid you're going to take my attention away from her. But the way I see it, none of us belongs to anyone, and anyone belongs to no one. No one here is under contract, you're all free to come and go as you please. I don't own you." Bette put her hands at the nape of my neck and lifted my hair into a twist. She pinned the curls at the top of my head with a tortoiseshell pin and then placed one of her pillbox hats over my face. She brought the mesh veil down over my eyes and put a mirror in front of me so I could take a look.

"You know girls, my mother left me, too. Or, rather, she forced me out. She said that when she found out she was pregnant with me she felt like her entire body was set on fire. She ached from heartburn and a boiling belly. A midwife told her to chew licorice and caraway seeds to beat the heat. She went into labor at home, screaming so loudly the neighbor a mile down the road came running.

"My mother submerged herself in a tub of ice water, in the middle of January. Her lips went blue and never came back to a normal pink. As I exited her body, all the fire escaped, too. She cracked and spilled open, frigid and brittle, frightened by her loud and angry child. She was afraid I might melt her. *Fly away fly away fly away,* she would mutter to me when I came too near. She locked me in my room and slid food under my door to keep me alive. If I went hungry, she reasoned, I might eat her. When I hit puberty I burst like a deluge in horizontal directions. Boys took notice and I went khaki-wacky for them, too. I stopped reading and studying and focused on all the boys in my class. I jumped from bed to bed. One night, I found my mother sitting at the kitchen table waiting for me.

"She said, 'This is your last meal, time to go. I

can't be having a whore in my house anymore, people are talking.' That's what she said to me, can you believe it?

'Where am I supposed to go?' I asked.

'Try your grandma in Eureka, she said.

'I didn't know I had a grandma.'

'Everyone has a grandma.' The old wretch handed me a note with an address.

'How am I supposed to get there? I'm not even old enough to drive.'

'Why don't you get one of your gentleman callers to take you?' she said.

"So I called up Peter with the blue Chevrolet. I knew he'd be awake, since he'd just dropped me off after our date.

'Let's go tonight,' he said, still drunk.

"We drove up here to Sky-on-the-Lake that night, straight through. When we got here his drunk had worn off, along with his bravado. He said, 'I gotta go back, Betty, I can't get fired from another job. You know I'll always love you,' and shoved ten dollars in my hand. That was a lot back then and I didn't ask where he got it. He dropped me off at a diner and I asked the waitress for directions to my grandmother's house.

'That place? That place burned to the ground last year,' she said. But I went to the address anyway and found this here hotel. It wasn't in half-bad shape, so I rolled up my sleeves and fixed it up, and here we are. You see what I mean? Sometimes a loss can also be a gain, an opening to your calling."

"What happened to your grandma?" Esther

asked.

"Oh, I put her in a nice place where they could take care of her better than I ever could."

I wondered where this magical place was, where all problems went away, kiss 'em goodbye, and you needed no one to get through the day.

NOW WITH A SWING

You can learn a lot from eavesdropping. My goal was not to gather evidence of indiscretions on the part of others, but rather, evidence that they were thinking and talking about me. I wanted to hear their disappointment and vexation so that I had no reason to try to open up. If they didn't like me, I didn't have to like them. It was easier that way. In Sandpiper Springs, I had no privacy and no need to listen in on conversations. With nowhere to hide, there was nothing to hide. And for all her faults, my mother said what she meant and meant what she said, and we girls grew to take words to heart. My sisters were too self-absorbed to discuss anything other than themselves, or one another. Minny and Esther figured we were all the same, so if one of us was discussed, we all were discussed. If one of us messed up, we all messed up. If one of us did good, we all did good. But up north at Bette's, words were deceptive. The women we lived with used language as trickery, veiling their intentions in saccharine compliments or, conversely, dagger-sharp ridicule. The only solution to sift through this obscurity of meaning was to listen in on private conversations.

Dinner each night was followed by a social

hour in the parlor with nightcaps and tea. I took charge of serving at these gatherings, since June had too light of a touch on the booze for the effect that I wanted, and the other girls were too lazy for hospitality. I found that a few extra slogs did wonders for budding windbags. Bette never joined us at the after-dinner hour. She left her plate for us to clear and went to her office for "a few more hours of work." She stayed up long past the rest of us and usually slept through breakfast, sometimes lunch, awakening after the sun was mid-sky to give us notes on our routines. At the teas, the girls let loose, freed from Bette's hovering or questioning the caloric intake of a Brandy Alexander. As I poured, they lounged and slouched, teased and flirted. A little extra for Kiki, a bonus for Blanca, a supplement for everyone to make my monkey business simple.

"I'm beat."

"Time to hit the sack."

"I think you mean the hay."

"Looks like you could use a little extra beauty sleep."

"Oh, can it."

Off they'd go to their rooms, feigning exhaustion, but I knew better. They may have been drained from the activity of the group, but they still needed their fill of more intimate, and juicy, conversation. June and Kiki, Blanca and Charlene, Franny alone, and my two sisters. I waited for Esther and Minny to fall asleep (which never took long, none of us ever had any trouble resting) and then snuck off to snoop. For the most part, the gossip was banal—hopes and dreams for the future (husband, kids, silver screen fame). But peppered in-between these heartfelt confessions were tidbits of information I could use to piece together how the girls felt about me.

She's odd, cold, shallow, amateur. They all look and sound the same, what's so special about her? I think the audience is bored by her. I'm bored by her. They're a gimmick. Flashes in the pan. They're good, but not great. Sounds like you're jealous. Who do they think they are? Waltzing in here all pre-teen with no manners, thinking they own the place? I think they're sweet. They're a bit clueless, if you ask me. If you want my opinion. To my mind.

Words to justify my distance and any required action.

One night after my famous extra-strong Yaka Hula Hickey Dulas sent everyone to bed, I crouched low at the crack between my bedroom door and the floorboards, and noticed the edge of June's pajama set sneak toward Bette's room. A *tap tap tap* with the knuckle of her bony hand. Bette appeared still fully dressed in her smoking suit, her hair still in place, but her wingtips replaced by furry red slippers with gold tassels. She placed her arm around June's shoulder and pulled her in, shutting the door behind her. I took a chance and snuck down the hall to sit furtive at Bette's closed door. I'd tried this before, but as she was usually alone, there wasn't much to hear. She kept her door locked so I couldn't rifle through her papers, neither (not the case for Franny, who kept detailed diaries, mostly containing plans for moving east to escape showbiz all together).

On the Hula Hickey night, I heard Bette chattering away in a what sounded like a one-sided conversation about two actors famous for their rivalry on-screen and off. Something about "using their hatred to my advantage." Once you got that woman talking, she was known to yap, but, unprompted, she appeared taciturn. Then the night went quiet and the light clicked off, but no one exited the room. I couldn't resist the effects of my weak Hickey any longer and took to bed. For the all the nights that followed, I kept my eye on June. Mostly she went off with Kiki, to slander the rest of the girls in the house. But on the nights she refused a third round, I made sure to watch for her feet at Bette's threshold, to listen in on their conversation. Were they plotting against us all? What news was June feeding Bette? The silence of the room was the most disconcerting information of all.

In the Sandpiper Springs Trailer Park, I had observed our mare with similar incredulity. I threw pinches of salt over my left shoulder every time I saw her. The silence of the horse Pearl troubled me—I couldn't read the beast. So much trust went into our relationship, I needed some words of affirmation. How could I be sure she wouldn't buck me? She was an ancient creature, greying at the muzzle and along her spine. Her right eye was opaque from blindness and her left eye was all penetrating pupil. I saw my face reflected in this good eye, distorted to an ovoid with a rainbow cast. No matter how many hundreds of times I brushed her mane, her hair would not take a shine. Maggie taught us to braid her tail to keep it free of brambles and knots, and we requested the same hairdo for ourselves. Pearl was too old to trot, let alone gallop, and spent her day meandering around her pen, chewing on the oats we threw to the ground. Still, confronted by such heft, I feared her kickback. There was still some buck in that creature and I had a feeling it would be my burden to bear. Maggie supervised my sisters and me as we took turns riding Pearl around the edge of the fence. She threw a serape over Pearl's back to soak up her sweat but my pants were still soaked through after I dismounted. The smell of horse shit, along with rose, plastic, and hot cocoa with freeze-dried marshmallows, still transports me to the past.

The Cuckoo used to keep an old sepia photograph of herself as a young girl riding Pearl. In the photo she was astride the galloping horse, her legs flying off the ground, her lips peeled in a smile from ear-to-ear. I cannot accept that an animal can change so considerably from the passage of time. That I can't ever know what animals are thinking drives me absolutely mad. They could be plotting anything, so one must remain alert.

I could tell the other girls were getting restless, and that our arrival wasn't the only reason. Around the table I saw us all as a tableau of squirming bodies, the eight of us twitching, picking at scabs, hangnails, napkins; mashing food with the back of utensils; gnashing teeth and tongues; shifting weight from one side to the other and back again; scratching chins, foreheads, earlobes, kneecaps; twiddling toes; eyes darting from one left to right; lips licking; voices lashing out anecdote after anecdote after non sequitur in a pointless, seamless stream. The show hadn't been on the road in years, despite Bette's endless promises and plans. The routines were hackneyed and the other girls in the house barely practiced anymore, spending their off-hours playing cards or fussing at their vanities.

Bette noticed the tension, too, of course. She had a hawk's eye for the most subtle emotional shifts. "Let's fix up the trailer and go on a summer tour up and down the coast, what do you say? We'll hit all the spots: San Francisco, Seattle, Reno, Las Vegas, then south to Los Angeles. Maybe even Mexico."

"Margaritas by the beach, Bette?" June made a face that betrayed that she had heard this promise once or twice before.

"Anything goes if we work hard enough this season. Our Christmas show could bring in a pretty penny, if we market ourselves right."

"Why don't you put the Starlings on the job? They've got their routine down pat, plenty of free time for them to gussy up the old jalopy."

Bloody June.

The trailer was a warped wooden catastrophe tucked under a tarp in the backyard. When we removed the sheath, hundreds of brown bumped bugs hopped and scattered to the garden. The paint was peeling in corkscrews. The wheels were in need of tires and realignment.

"What a disaster," Minny said, kicking the bumper. She left no dent. Despite appearances, this was a sturdy chariot.

"Let's paint it red, that'll hide the cosmetic damage," Esther was applying some rouge she had "liberated" from the back of Franny's dresser drawer. "Red, with blue and white stripes, for an Independence Day show."

Bette tossed us a few bills for the renovation. "Let's do it on the cheap," I suggested. "Save the money for later." We gathered paint and bedding and fabrics from discarded costumes and sets to cover the interior. Minny stenciled a white star on other side of the trailer with our show's new name in jumbo black letters: BETTE'S GREAT 8 TOM TOM REVUE. At the back she painted bursting fireworks.

"So that when we leave, it's like we're the explosion," she explained.

We arranged everything so it was built to move, or could be stored in multiple arrangements. We hinged a ramp out the back that could be propped up as a teaser stage, hung a metal rod across the long end of the interior to hang our costumes, installed two seated benches with extra storage under the cushions. Blanca came to help, once the heavy labor was finished, to add some homey touches and potpourri made of sage and bay leaves from a tree in the yard.

When we were finished we sent for Bette and waited for her judgment.

"Girls, you never cease to amaze me. What can't you do? It looks fantastic, though the color scheme may be a bit irrelevant for our trip."

"I thought you said we were leaving in the summer? I figured it'd be good for the Fourth of July." Esther really didn't have the skin for criticism. I hated to see my baby sister curdle.

"I have some exciting news, very exciting. I was going to wait until dinner to tell everyone but now is as good a time as any. I've made arrangements with the owner of the Peep and Squeal in Colton City and, guess what girls? We'll be performing our Christmas show there instead! It's a real first-class joint and I know it'll bring in a lot of new faces. We'll do a full week, Christmas through New Year's. Isn't that terrific?"

"But Bette, we always do the Christmas show here. Folks love it."

"Kiki, one has to keep things fresh if one hopes to survive in this business. Things change before you can deliver your one-two. If I know anything about audiences—and I know *everything* about audiences—they want to be kept on their toes. We'll charge double for the show, with a discount if you buy both a Christmas and a New Year's Eve ticket. Just think, the idea of missing their beloved end-of-year show will not only get folks to explore a new locale, but they'll also throw down more bucks to see us do what we do best."

"Will we still do a summer tour?"

"Let's see how this trip pans out, Charley, and then we'll decide on a longer trip. Who knows, maybe we'll attract so many new faces to Bunting House we won't need a tour!"

The next day Bette woke my sisters and me before anyone else.

"Girls, I have a special treat for you, for all your hard work." She dangled the keys to her convertible.

Bette taught us to drive that day, in the parking lot of the diner off the highway. We each took turns at the wheel, tentative pushes on the gas and quick releases of the clutch sending us all jolting upright out of our seats. Folks out after Sunday services stumbled out from the diner with bellies full of hotcakes and syrup, and had to dash out of the way of our veering automobile, rushing home with indigestion.

Minny was the quickest to pick up the trick.

"Why don't you drive us to dairy bar, I'll buy us a treat." Bette was leaning her arm out the passenger side, smoking a cigarette. She rambled on again about her dreams for the show, the same promises about going to Chicago and all the way to New York, the places to be if you wanted a stage show. She said if we made enough money at the Peep and Squeal, we could hit St. Louis, Omaha, New Orleans. And then: we'd go international.

"Maybe we could team up with some jazz groups down there. You ever been to New Orleans?

Fabulous town, girls, you'd love it."

"We've never left California, Bette," I said, gripping my seat with my fingernails.

"It's high time that changed! Maybe we won't even come back." She flicked the cigarette out the window, sending it shooting backwards toward the empty road behind us.

CHEEK TO CHEEK

We left two weeks before Christmas so we'd arrive and have plenty of time for rehearsal. Minny sat in the passenger seat next to Bette, chatting up a storm, and taking turns at the wheel. When she wasn't driving she was picking Bette's brain about the ins-and-outs of the business, taking notes on a small flip-ledger she'd bought with a secret tip. Esther fussed over herself in a small hand mirror. She tucked the same pin-curl behind her ear repeatedly, and applied and reapplied lipstick the color of a piggy-bank. She obsessed over her color chart and claimed the lighter hues suited her facial tone. Before bed each night she practiced facial distortions, claiming it would prevent wear and tear. The rest of us sat in the trailer playing cards, pinochle, spades, and vingt-et-un.

"Hit me. Hit me. Hit me" became the mantra of our voyage.

"Esther, Esther, Esther," I called my sister's attention away from her ointment application ritual.

She waited to finish her twentieth clockwise circle on her forehead before blinking at me.

"Yes, Pearl?"

"Wanna play?"

"Not now, I still have to work on my foundation."

We arrived in Colton City at a quarter-to-four. The Peep and Squeal was a timber-framed mansion dressed with stone, massive beams, and a joist for every post. Peppermint icing scrollwork and fretwork decorated the eaves of the high windows. Sugar gumdrop stairways led a pathway inside. The doors were made of gingerbread, the grounds guarded by gnomes camouflaged as shrubs manicured in the shape of lollipops.

"Maybe a fairy will prep our stage," Esther needled me.

"Yeah, a little glitter greenie will descend from the rafters and arrange our costumes all in a row." Minny spoke with her hands, waggling her fingers and then spreading an imaginary wardrobe in front of my face. She pinched my nose and I pinched hers back.

The building had been erected over a river. The architect shared a deep affection for the local flora and fauna and so built the structure around the waterway. The stream flowed through the center of the building, cutting the main lounge in half. Visitors had to walk across a small bridge to get from one side of the building to the other. Check-in, the bar, and a receiving area were on the side near the main entrance. The stage and our sleeping quarters were on the other. A regal bay tree grew in the main hall, cutting through a skylight that let in the light from a few stars and a slice of the moon.

The back of the building was less of a dream.

The manager had converted a shared bathroom into a dressing area for the performers. He'd nailed wooden disks to the top of a defunct toilet as a seating area and installed a knobby rug that stunk of wet towels. So too were our hopes for an inspiring performance area squashed. The stage was in a triangular room, shoved in a corner and elevated mere inches from the sitting area. There was no curtain.

Blanca was livid. "How are we gonna have a curtain call with no curtain?"

"How are we going to do the hatbox trick?" Minny asked.

"Don't be so high and mighty. This place is the tits. Starlings, you can do another trick, I'm sure you have it in you," June said.

"Is this place too good for you?" I whispered to Esther.

She shot me a frothy smile and pinched my arm.

"That's nonsense! I'll perform anywhere and for anyone, even a colony of ants."

"So they'd make you their queen?"

Her smile turned to a blazing look, a flicker of awareness, followed by another pinch, this time on my bare cheek.

"I'm beelining for the bar," she said. "Who's with me?"

I said no but followed Esther to the bar, peeking from behind a chintzy curtain. Bette sat perched on a stool sipping Manhattans and smoking one du Maurier after another du Maurier. She was wearing a floor-length red velvet dress with leopard print gloves. The smoke from her cigarettes circled Esther's head like vultures. She ran her thumbnail against her lip, deep in thought.

"Whisky," Esther ordered.

The bartender looked at my sister askance. "How old are you?"

"Oh just give the girl a drink, Al, she deserves her comp." Bette waved the bartender's practicality away with her gloved hand, and Al poured a double and two more, one for himself and one for Bette.

"Cheers."

"Thanks for the drink," Esther said.

"You deserve it. You can dance, but can you sing? It's a twofer that really makes the bill."

"Sure, I can sing," Esther said, beginning to break into song. Bette put her hand on her mouth.

"I'll believe it when I hear it," she laughed. I loved her laugh, it was quick and rattling and cut to the point.

"Want another drink?" She reached across the bar for the bottle and poured herself a finger full in a tiny glass, clinked in a couple of ice cubes from a bucket, and plopped in two cherries plucked from a crinkle-edged bowl.

I went to bed but when I woke, I found my sister Esther asleep next to me, wrapped in Bette's mink coat.

❋

Colton City was a misty town tucked between two large cities to the north and south. People came for the mountain escape, the vistas, the peace and quiet, and some came for the famous pie from a greasy spoon called Rusty's. There was no big-city gilded gleam here, no hustle-bustle. The men in town were rowdier than our crowd back home. They were more hungry, more bored. They meandered toward the stage, frothing at the mouth, spitting compliments our way. The drinks up here were more stiff, too. Bette rigged up a system to protect us from the advances of these hulking and pickled men. We were to tip our beers on the sly into a hidden trough that ferried our empty bottles back to the kitchen where they were re-bottled and re-sold to the very men who were out there on the floor trying to win our favor but who were losing it to the booze.

On Christmas morning, Minny sliced us pepperoni, mozzarella, and pears for breakfast. For a little privacy we made a fort on the side of the wagon with our blanket and a few chairs pulled from the lobby.

"I think we should perform our 'Angels in Heaven' routine. I found this old pillow batting and golden wire in the costume kit," Esther said.

"We can sing 'Cheek to Cheek,'" Minny said. "*Heaven … I'm in Heaven.*" She piled her slice of pear high with dappled fatty meat and, wide-eyed, swallowed the tower in one full gulp.

"IwanoobeeFreAstaire," she said, her mouth

full of food

I grabbed the paring knife and sliced a bit of cheese.

"Don't talk with your mouth full, no one can understand a word you're saying."

We were due for a matinee that day, Bette didn't believe in taking holidays. Christmas, Thanksgiving, New Year's Eve and Day, now that's where the money was. People at home were hankering for a breath of fresh air away from family time. Fathers went out running ambiguous errands for hours on end—missing batteries, forgotten lemons, gassing up the car. We'd been working another new routine for a few weeks, a symposium. I had mentioned our old game with the Cuckoo offhand one night at dinner and Bette thought it'd make a splendid show. She wrote a script and handed it to us with not much time to memorize. We were all to dress up like Greek goddesses and sing on the recline.

"Some think reclining is the pose of the lazy, the elite, or the chosen few who don't have to attend to work or children. But to recline need not be bourgeoise. Nor is it a passive pose. Greek men did all their plotting and planning, their boasting, their eating and drinking from the recline at the original symposia. In those days it was considered downright rude to sit upright at the dinner table during these gatherings. Imagine if our modern-day politicians met to discuss international conflict, law, and order on the 'kline. The dialogue might actually be civilized, and the outcome practical. Oh, and girls, don't forgot to mention our travel sponsor, Barcalounger."

Bette threw scripts at us, along with some fabric for togas.

The eight of us drooped over eight horizontal surfaces–a Barcalounger, a towel, two pillows, a low table, a prop windowsill, a princess bed, and an army cot. We wore togas made from thread-worn sheets (printed with fading bluebells or chic stripes, one a gaudy red silk). We all held the pose of someone recovering from a faint. Blanca broke the dead air.

"I am an uncluttered arrangement of limbs. Reclining is effortless and, as a result, so is reclined thinking. In repose pose one dreams and one relaxes. Your muscles don't have to work nearly as hard as when you're standing upright, so your brain can really start to exercise."

June spoke next.

"Think of the rejuvenating principles of sleep. Now think of that same feeling of rejuvenation working on you while you're awake. Oh, if only you reclined more often! How very refreshed you would feel!"

Charlene took it now.

"How softly you would react to stress! One can't be brittle lying down. To lie down is to be receptive."

Esther now.

"To recline is to be at one's most natural position. Children spend hours reclining outside on hills, looking up at the sky, finding patterns in cloud formations."

Minny at bat.

"They test their eyes against the blare of the sun or imagine themselves as birds."

My turn.

"At night, they lie down in woods or in back-yards (if there are no woods), and stargaze, hoping to catch a glimpse of a shooting star, or better yet, a UFO."

Back to Kiki.

"When upright, your thoughts can only shoot forward. You're left thinking, what's next? What's ahead of me? Reclining allows the mind to reach the moon."

Franny showed a drawing of the moon. She drew a sleeping lady in one of the moon's craters. We had by then taken notice of one another.

Blanca, speaking a bit louder this time. "Looking down is just as effortless as looking up. Your line of vision while reclining is all shins and feet. Have you ever meticulously, scrupulously, assiduously observed your own feet? If you're like most people, probably not. But try it out—there's a whole other world waiting for you to explore right there on your feet!"

Franny held up a drawing of a pair of feet. One foot wore a ballet slipper, the other wore a men's nighttime loafer.

June grabbed the drawing and clutched it to her chest.

"There is peace at the end of your body. If you're holding anything while lying down, the thing must be held very close to your chest. Thus, very close to your heart. That could make the thing more precious."

Charlene reached over and stole the paper from June. She laid it across her forehead like a cool towel.

"Take breakfast in bed. Doesn't breakfast in bed taste better than it does crouched over a lousy desk? If you drink your coffee too fast or eat your eggs too quickly, you'll probably stain your bed-sheets. Therefore, it is best to pick at your food while lying down, so you'll most likely never get fat, making up for the lack of exercise you do not do when in repose."

Fran held up a drawing of breakfast. Fried eggs and buttered toast and coffee. A Belgian waffle with syrup and blackberries and a swirl of whipped cream. Charlene ditched the drawing of the feet and snatched this one instead.

Minny jumped in, this time she was off cue.

"I imagine tranquility aids with digestion, as well."

Franny presented a drawing of intestines. The pink labyrinthine tube grew into cobra heads at either end.

We all sat up at this line, pitched forward toward one another.

"And smarts, too! Words from books adhere to your memory better from this position because you must actively stay awake."

Esther. She was so coy with the delivery of her lines.

"To recline is a feminist act. The reposed figure refuses to defer to the erect."

"Horizontality is a position of absorption."

Now we spoke all at once. Our voices over-lapped and we fought to have our lines heard amongst the din.

"It collapses walls, an offense to the verticality of patriarchal hierarchies."

"To recline is to flatten the playing field."

Franny showed a picture of a cleat kicking a football over the goal post.

Charlene fell asleep. June tore at the sheets beneath her, Kiki grabbed the picture of the football and gnawed at the edges, and we the Starlings wrestled for center stage. Blanca interrupted the chaos.

"To recline is to evoke the sensual, while denying the behind. The reclining position allows a woman to size her opponent up with stealth. All from the safety of her Barcalounger."

Franny stepped up and presented a poster ad for Barcalounger: "Left blooming alone? All your lovely companions faded and gone? Kick back in a Barcalounger and reflect on your blushes, give a sigh for a sigh!" Kiki read the ad like a grammar lesson on a chalkboard.

My turn. I'd almost forgot to speak with my body at high alert.

"Does the recline remind you of the womb? Good, it should, because you were reclining in there as well. And look how well that turned out. You were reclining from the beginning and you will, most likely, recline at the end. The middle parts are as good a time as any to relax."

We were all covered in sweat from repressed rage. The surfaces of the stage were upturned. Our reclining beds and chairs were toppled and ravaged. I struggled to catch my breath and forgot I had my sister, not sure which one, in a headlock.

Bette clapped with vigor from her seat. "Well done! But Charlene, dear, I think you should pop in a bit more, yes? Perhaps say something from the depths of dreamland? And all of you, give me more agitation, more embellishment. Starlings, what if you pretended to suffocate one another with a pillow? And Fran, maybe you rumple the paper and throw it at Charlene to wake her up? Let's try it from the top."

Bette had us practice the routine until Blanca "accidentally" tore a bit too hard at Kiki's hair, pulling out a chunk and sending the girl, in tears, to walk it off around the perimeter of the building. I didn't take my eyes off Esther, who appeared too nonchalant for the day's activities. The rest of us were panting and spent. Once we were rested and fed, Bette announced our lineup for the Christmas Eve show.

"We're starting with the opening song, that's with everyone. I think we'll do 'Moonlight Cocktail,' since we're playing on tips. '*Couple of jiggers of moonlight and add a star. Pour in a June night,* and June, here you'll step forward and do a solo, *and one guitar,* that's your cue Kiki, *mix in a couple of dreamers,* the rest of you step forward in line again, *and there you are: Lovers hail the Moonlight Cocktail.* And then cheers to the audience and pretend to drink your champagne, but girls, it's just soda water tonight. Then we move to:

Act One: Knives and Flames, Blanca
Act Two: Comedy, June
Act Three: Pantomime, Franny
Act Four: Charlene and Franny's pas-de-deux
Act Five: Contortionists, the darling Starlings
Act Six: Grande finale

"We'll end with more comedy. I think we should do the new one tonight, to test the crowd."

"What about my act?" Kiki was dressed in a luxurious gown of gold sequins—she'd painted her face with faux gold dust powder.

"I don't think it's ready, Kiki dear. Or I should say that the crowd isn't ready for you. Besides, we have to cut the act short tonight, there's some big band on stage after us as top billing. You'll be shining bright in the opening and closing, I'm sure of it." Kiki's golden face drained of color. She huffed and made her way to the door.

"Kiki, we still need you for the finale. It won't be the same without you." Bette called after her. She turned and rejoined our group, sliding her body down the wall to a crouched position. I felt her glare dig into my back.

Though we were billed as family-friendly, our audiences were normally made up of men—an even split of passers-through and small-town regulars who came for the drinks and stayed for the show. You could count on at least one night of big spenders, men's conferences or consortiums. Usually this happened on a Tuesday, when the whole place could be booked for a large party. Bette said most folks liked to drink on Tuesdays because they had dried out from the weekend on Monday, but now that the work week undeniably stretched out in front of them, they were ready for another drink.

"Tuesdays are a real gas," she said. "Day two of the work week and folks are already anxious to add a little fun to the humdrum."

Fridays were family nights, a good chance to get the kids out of the house since there wasn't school the next day and Mom and Pop were too beat from the doldrums to get really decked out for the night. On Fridays we kept it polite and respectable with lots of physical comedy, slapstick, and banana jokes. High brow content in a low brow joint. Saturdays were the real fun. Folks had spent the day away from the desk, running around with the kids, or just plain relaxing and were now ready to get dolled up, soused, and spend their hard-earned cash. The kids were safely tucked in at home with babysitters. Besides, a little hangover at Sunday service took the edge off the sermons.

On Saturdays we played two shows: an early-bird special (two tickets for the price of one-and-a-half!) for the older crowd and the kiddies and teens. The late show was after dinnertime, nine-thirty or so, depending on the audience trickle. These were the shows at which we could get riskier or risqué. Those shows ran into the wee hours of the morning, encores after encores, until two, three, even four o'clock, until the cops came and put a kibosh on the good times. Our curfew went out the window if people were still buying drinks. Usually, the boys in blue would stick around too—long enough to see an act and have a drink, or sometimes join us for our after-work meal, a night-owl roast and toast followed by welcome sleep. We were up again a few hours later to get dressed and do it all over again.

On the first Saturday at the Peep, a man with a rawboned face, chrome-domed, and clad all in black entered the showroom. He sat with an older gentleman, a handsome man with a swath of thick grey hair. The man wore a fine oxford shirt with cufflinks shaped like toads. His shoes were polished to a blinding shine. The older man laughed a loud and infectious guffaw, turning heads each time he opened his floppy mouth. The younger man smirked now and again, but otherwise remained mute.

After the shows I watched the men slink backstage to Bette's office. I followed them down to eavesdrop but found Esther had beaten me to the punch. I pressed my body against the corner of the wall to hide. The younger man caught Esther on her knees at the doorstep, on his way back from the loo.

"You're one of the Starlings, aren't you? Your act was very impressive, sweetheart. Here, why don't you take my card. If you're ever in Los Angeles, give me a buzz. Did anyone ever tell you look like a young...oh, what's her name? That red head? You know who I'm talking about. She's It right now. Anyway, here's a tip." He tucked a rumpled bill in her pocket and knocked to enter Bette's office.

The man's words rung in my ears. Was she the most talented one? She seemed like she didn't give a hoot. Were my sisters and I not all equal slices of pie, like I had grown up thinking? My whole life I felt even-steven with my sisters, perfect thirds. I grabbed for memories that could lead me to the truth and landed on a banal image of the Cuckoo and I clearing dishes from the cabana. She caught my hand as I ate scraps from the plates.

"When you were a baby, you grabbed the food first, you know that? You clawed for my breast and stole my nipple straight out from under your sisters. Some might think that's greedy but I think it's shrewd. Do you know what that word means? Shrewd? It means you're thinking for the future. There might not be enough to go around, but you make sure you have enough. Stay hungry."

I skipped breakfast the next day and walked into town to see the latest box office flick, but I had hours to spare before the first showing. I found the money left-over from the jalopy rehab in my pocket and stopped at a drug store for red hair tint. I dyed my hair the color of a pumpkin in the bathroom while everyone else was still asleep.

"What have you done?" Minny cried.

"You've ruined our act," Esther said. "Typical Pearl."

"I think I'll remind people of that young redhead-ed starlet. The It girl. It's good to mix it up, that's what Bette always says."

"We're all supposed to look the same. That's the point of our entire schtick."

But Bette stood up for me when all the girls were up in arms.

"I think Pearl has a point. Three Goldilocks sisters were once cute, but it's wearing thin on our audience. It's time for a little more variety in this variety show. Think of it as a relationship of differences."

"I have a suggestion." June was leaning against the threshold to the bathroom, waiting to put on her face. "How about Minny, you dye your hair black, and Esther, you go platinum."

"Wonderful idea, June! What do you say girls?"

"I even have some bleach lying around," June said. "My just-in-case bleach."

"Fantastic, have it ready for tonight."

June put down her toiletries and pushed my sisters to sit on the counter. She tugged at Esther's hair.

"Minny, yours will be easy, it's always easy to go dark. But Esther, oh, sweetie, this is going to sting, your hair is real thick."

Minny and I left the bathroom, pinching our noses from the stench and escaping the howls of our baby sister. She emerged, coated in crusted tears, with a luxurious, if a bit less than silky, head of white hair.

"You look just like a blonde bombshell!" Blanca cooed.

"You're all different and somehow that makes you less special. Funny how that works." June was twirling her soiled plastic gloves and admiring her handiwork. "A duck ain't a chicken and a chicken ain't a wren, but they're still all just birds."

A MOMENT MORE AND SHE WILL FLY

Things were tense that final night at the Peep and Squeal. It was New Year's Eve so expectations were high, from both sides of the stage. Even Bette was more uptight than usual, though she tried to remain outwardly upbeat. What's worse, all the acts were falling flat. Blanca couldn't hit her high notes and cut her finger on a thumb-spin knife trick. She kept performing despite the blood spurting until she went faint and Charlene had to rescue her with some quip about getting axed. Twice Kiki broke her violin strings. When it came time for our act—we were to be the last before the finale that night—the audience was visibly and audibly restless. There was no cheering or clapping, merely the awkward clinking of glasses in a silent room.

We were to perform our ode to the Cuckoo, an act we called "Birds of a Feather," in which we dressed as tropical birds on a lifeguard watch. I had begged my sisters to change the routine, I didn't have all the moves down yet.

"Can't we do the old hatbox trick? People love that one."

"Pearl, don't worry. We always pull through. It's easier with an audience, the pressure makes you perform better. You know this." It was easy for Esther to say, everything came easy to her. On this particular day, however, a portent awaited me on my settee. Kiki had bungled our costumes, folding Esther's toucan dress on my seat at the vanity. The costumes were heavy with baubles, I needed two arms to lift the getup and rehang it neatly on Esther's side of the room. As I did, a slip of paper fluttered to the floor. On one side was a date, an appointment, and an address in Hollywood. On the other side, written in blue ballpoint, was a note: *To Esther, looking forward to chatting with you more. You're the star of the show, and we could use more stars like you in this town. Signed, X.*

"This show is cursed," I said. What a way to go out, with a fizz rather than a bang. I threw her costume at her and took back my own.

At first, it seemed Esther was right. We were nailing all our moves. The pressure of outside eyes did make our performance a cut above the rest. All fear was put on hold when the spotlight hit our faces. We moved around one another without flaw. We tied our arms and legs in knots and hit our notes while topsy-turvy. We undulated in alternating and repetitive movements to mimic a kaleidoscope. First you have to hook 'em…my father's advice. Lifts and turns and twirls and spins to make us appear in flight. The audience was perking up, too. At first they sent us gun-shy claps but once we did the first dandy acrobatic, they were more confident in their laughter. Upside down in a mid-air arabesque, the sound of rain on the rooftop sounded like tap shoes on the floor.

For our final trick, we were to climb to the top of a large prop coconut tree. Esther had wanted us to fly down after our crescendo, but Bette said the money for a rigging for such a trick was not in our budget. Instead, Esther came up with a sort of shimmy move up the trunk of the tree. We'd grab coconuts and joggle them in front of our bust-lines while we finished our song:

> *Straighten up and fly right*
> *Straighten up and fly right*
> *Straighten up and fly right*

If we hooked our thighs around the base, we could use each other's arms to move up to the top as a threesome, where we could lean back and finish our falsettos. We cooed and cawed and whistled. Our feathers spread, revealing opulent plumage. The rain was coming through the ceiling. A droplet fell in my open mouth as I reached a high octave on the word extraordinary. The audience was protecting their heads from the water with their cloth napkins.

Esther improvised.

"My, how very tropical! Our very own rainforest!"

This cracked the audience out of their seats. They stood to watch the three exotic creatures high up in their coconut tree.

Before the song ended we were supposed to

shift our bodies out, with only our feet supporting us on the tree, our hands clasped to form a human ringlet around the trunk. Minny made sure to check the tree before we went up. "Ten times," she said she checked it. It was sturdy, there was no doubt. Backstage, the rest of the girls were holding it steady with extra anchors, just in case.

Esther was sweating profusely. She was pale.

How very, extraordinary.

I was so high from the energy of the audience on this bittersweet final show of the year, our first year in the revue. I didn't notice Esther was no longer holding my hand. I didn't notice the music had stopped, the audience had stopped their cheering, and Minny was no longer singing but screaming—I was dangling from the branch, held up by Minny's arm. She was clinging to the tree with her other arm and looking down at the stage. Below our tree lay our little toucan, her neck bent in a way that even we had never practiced. A bit of blood trickled from her lip. Her feathers covered her face like a shield. The audience was murmuring as Bette barked for the curtains to close.

CALLBACKS

Tough love, time to grow up, time to move on, you can't stay in this business forever. Bodies break down, you meet someone, you fall in love, get married, have kids. You have to be practical, what's so wrong with being ordinary? One can't entertain beyond one's own mortality, after all. Every movement becomes mechanized. Life is fully predictable. Besides, no one likes an aging starlet. Pushing twenty, thirty, forty, fifty. The word we used was "routine." The numbers kept us going, the numbers maintained.

When the eight of us were together, Bette insisted we have both breakfast and dinner as a family. She said it kept us grounded but I suspected she really wanted to keep an eye on our diets. We were told to be sensible. Use moderation. Avoid all fried foods, rich soups, or anything containing flour or potatoes. You know, the starches. Abstain from alcohol. Drink enough caffeinated beverages to suppress hunger but not so much that you stain your teeth. Breakfast should be a light meal of a single slice of bacon, fruit, one egg, and a slice of dry toast. Lunch: a generous helping of salad and a bit of cheese. Dinner came in varying meats and vegetables and a tiny sweet. We were to enjoy the bitter foods, like olives, coffee, and lettuce.

Of course, most of the girls besides me snuck Hershey bars in their rooms, bottles of liquor, and Oreos. When we went to town, everyone got milk-shakes while I ordered a diet fountain soda. Most times I skipped the trips to town and spent the day shadowing Bette instead. I learned to schmooze, woo, and lick. How to build clientele, promote my image and assemble a portfolio.

The day Esther fell, after the cops showed up and shut the show down, after Esther was sent to the hospital with a concussion, a bruised face, and five knocked-out teeth, a shattered left leg (nine places), and hip (four), after everyone retired to bed, I stayed up with Bette, counting the books.

"Tonight was our most successful night of the run," she said. "Shame it's our last."

Bette poured me a bowl of raisin bran and just enough milk to cover, but not drown, the delicate flakes. I watched as she picked the raisins, one by one, out of her bowl. She set them aside on a napkin. "You're growing upper-lip hair. You know that?" She ran her finger under my nose. "That thing has got to go."

It was my job to count and pack up the cos-tumes: four boas, nine sequined gowns, ten pom-padour hats, eleven wigs (natural blonde, bleach blonde, bobbed girl-next-door brunette, pixie, ash, atomic red, auburn, mermaid blue, black-as-night, mellow yellow, creature-feature green, distinctive grey), twenty heels, twenty flats, seamed and seam-less tights, an Egyptian atef, two tuxedos (trim), two wing-tips, a set of tap shoes, a top hat, eight corselettes and girdle sets, the togas, the codpieces, a feathered cap, cane, parasol, and a rubber nose. The girls all kept track of their own makeup.

Minny and I were with Esther when she woke in the hospital bed after days of unconsciousness. She was at first silent and then she was yelling for a nurse— Who? What? Where? I'm awake, I'm awake! She didn't notice Esther and I in the corner. And then she did and she touched her own face.

"What do you remember, Esther?" I asked before the nurse arrived.

"The last thing I remember was hanging upside down with the skull of a coconut in my mouth and then something about a ripped toucan costume rumpled on the floor. And then I must have fallen asleep because I woke in this strange room, spare and sterile, where an identical version of me slept in a chair in the corner. Another woman who looked nothing like me was awake beside me. The girl who looked like me awoke and ran to me, she called me Esther."

"Do you know your name?"

"Esther Starling, sister to Pearl and Minny. Daughter to Georgia, aka the Cuckoo." It all came rushing back to Esther, I could see it in her eyes— lights, cheers, bows, sequins, lipstick, whisky sours, whisky sodas, ribbons, fake diamonds, and high heels. The out-of-body feeling of moving in a body.

"How long was I out?"

"Three days."

"Sheesh, what'd I miss?"

"Glad to see you still got your chutzpah." Minny kissed Esther on the cheek.

The doctors told Esther that she had a bum hip, that'd she'd probably never dance again. That she might be able to but really shouldn't, if she knew what was good for her.

"Esther Starling, still a teen and already an antique of the revue circuit." She calculated her remaining talents on the back of a hospital pulmonary health brochure: mediocre at singing, can sew some (buttons and hems), and cook some (meatloaf, baked chicken, enchiladas, coleslaw).

After she was released, we secured Esther in the back of the trailer for the ride home, by rigging her to a cot on top of the bench. The rest of us spent excruciating hours kneeling on the floor. No one spoke for the hours long ride back to Sky-on-the-Lake. Franny and June played cards in the corner. Bette gunned it home with Minny in the front seat beside her. Blanca was practicing her rouge application on Charlene. And I sat bolt upright in the back, my fists stuffed in my pockets, fidgeting with that appointment card at the bottom.

"Looks like you're gonna have to learn to do a duet," June said. Her breath stank like canned sardines. I waved her and the stench away.

Esther's long fall had mirrored, some said precipitated, our entire troupe falling short. Of making the rent, of attracting new audiences, of remaining germane. No matter how high we cut our skirts, how dumb we made our jokes, how many times we slashed our prices and cut our patrons deals, the numbers kept plummeting, down, down, down, into the red. With Hollywood's grip in full force, and instant entertainment making their way into the every-man's home, the revue was on its last leg when we joined. The stars of the stage and radio would rather be pioneers of primetime all on seven-inch television screens. Gee whiz, even television is a mime, stealing from the theater and the movies.

Things fizzled out quickly after our trip to the Peep and Squeal. I supposed the trip was a last-ditch effort by Bette to try to save an already sunken ship. I had to hand it to Bette—she managed to last longer than most small live theater owners thanks to family money and a disregard for debt. But even to my young mind it was becoming obvious that our senses of humor and puns were passé. In the eyes of our most faithful guests, we were shopworn. Bette began to disappear for even longer periods at a time, leaving Franny in charge. She directed us with drawings and emphatic gestures—an arm thrust toward dusty lampshades, a before and after charcoal of a trimmed hedge, a set of big Zzzzzzzzzzs. After heeding this drawing, we woke to find Franny had walked away. Her valise was gone, along with everyone's favorite jazz crooner record and the omelet-sized cast-iron pan. Each time Bette came back from raising funds, finding sponsors, securing venues, whatever it was she was doing, someone was missing. Pop pop pop, like shooting ducks at the fair, the women in the show dropped out. Down to Hollywood to make it big, test it out, be discovered. Out to Reno to hit the casinos and clubs. Way up north to forget it all. Walked off into the sunset, our narratives stuck in a formulaic loop.

June was the next to go after Franny. She had stopped creeping up to Bette's room when we returned from Colton City. When Bette left, she went to bed early and alone. Her routines became diminished of energy, as if performed by an empty clamshell. Her jokes were flat, boring, and missed all the marks. She called them her "unrequited jokes."

"If a heart is so apt to break, why keep it in such a fragile container? Why not try plastic?"

"A broken heart insinuates the possibility for repair. Can't we just save up and buy a new one?"

"No, broken is the incorrect word. It's not broken, it's gone. Then the heart is no longer a thing that needs mending but a thing that needs finding."

"But June, how do you search for something without knowing the shape or size or matter of the thing?"

"There is a vague understanding of size: it must be smaller than your chest. It must fit behind and between your lungs. It must be large enough to pump blood to the size of your body. Perhaps you should start by measuring your body and working backwards. How large would your heart have to be to remain alive? Or, conversely, what's the smallest heart you could survive upon? There is also a vague shape, a roundish, smooth shape—hard edges would poke the body. And taste? Plum jam. The tactile feeling? Also plum jam, more to the point: a finger stuck in warm plum jam. A scent: ice. And then would come a festering putridity. So now you have an idea of what you are looking for and may end up in the peanut butter and jelly aisle of your supermarket."

These were strange routines that sent audiences shaking their heads and walking away in the middle of her sentences.

She had also stopped wearing makeup. Looking at her face was alarming. I'd never seen such large pores exposed on a woman. I'd never seen her eyes so puffy, her face so discolored.. I'd never seen uneven skin tones. She left to scrape together a life through a combination of a careers on the comedy circuit, and as a waitress in a cocktail bar. She would die young, at age forty-eight, from liver failure or alcohol poisoning or some death related to her love of liquor, unable to ever get her name in lights.

At the theater, she aged a thousand years in one week and shriveled to an old woman, then composted to the earth. I thought, now this, Pop, is time compressed. There was no more spitting disparagements in our faces. Instead, she infused us with her condemnation from the ground up. Her quick demise permeated our lives and rotted the rest of the routines until we had no roots to keep us transfixed in Sky-on-the-Lake.

Kiki and Charlene got offered a gig in Reno, playing on the burgeoning casino circuit there. I heard Charlene became quite rich and well-known—there was, apparently, a lot of money to be had in the not-quite-Las Vegas-but-almost entertainment industry. She dated several well-known and several unknown sharks and gangsters, threw lavish holiday parties, and sang and danced in the town's biggest New Year's Eve night show every year. Kiki was less successful. Her routine as the Tears of a Clown violinist didn't go over too well with the Reno hood-lum and men-with-money-to-spare crowd. She was axed early from her duet with Charlene. Both wom-en by then had grown tired of one another, anyway. Kiki was increasingly judgmental about Charlene's lifestyle, and Charlene thought Kiki was a wet blan-ket. So, Kiki took off to some small town in Neva-da and transformed her life. She went by Katherine. She started a music school for elementary-school-age children. She had a long affair with the wife of the school superintendent and mother to her star pianist.

Blanca had also made her way to Hollywood and onto a TV show about a mute comedy writer who works for an incompetent man named Adam in New York City. The show was titled, with much self-congratulation on the part of the producer, Big Adam's Apple. The show was a two-season sensa-tion. But as the third season got underway, audiences grew tired of watching an innocent young girl lose all the credit to an inept man. From there, she would land a small bit role on a late-night show for a few episodes. Rumor has it, she ran away with one of the camera men to Mexico.

It was only two months after the holiday trip that Bette had the saloon closed up and packed out.

"Girls," she said. "I've been offered a once in a lifetime opportunity to have my own television show. When your chance arrives, I suggest you leap and take it, too." There was no bang leading us out, just a goodbye.

"I thought you hated television," Esther said. She had bit her bottom lip so that it bled.

Bette said: "You're right, I do. But pop culture is a barometer of the national spirit. Americans want their men strong and smoky, and their women squeaky clean, or beautiful and dumb. A successful female comedian knows a smart woman isn't funny. A beautiful woman is only funny if she's dumb. An ugly woman is funny if she's smart. But an ugly woman cannot be dumb. And a beautiful, smart, funny woman would be too much, too dangerous, too threatening. I wanted to give us a final hurrah, or sit on the decision a bit longer to let it gestate, and to wait for contract negotiations to go through."

"Maybe we'll be back together someday. But I'm confident that it's not the end of the road for you three, you still have your youth." As parting gifts, Bette gave us all one-way tickets to Los Angeles and a piece of advice: "Stay alert and keep your looks up."

Bette was kind enough to let us stay a few days while we figured out where to go. We spread out in the empty house. Every word we spoke echoed off the ceiling and bounced back to the floorboards. Minny and I attempted some duets but they all were missing that certain something. A duet wasn't all that special, but now, a trio… there was a sight. You ain't seen nothin' yet. They'll go bananas. We were the talk of the town, not so long ago.

"I'm dead weight," Esther said after it'd been weeks since the accident and she still couldn't get up without our help. We were sitting on the porch waiting for the right moment to leave. She flexed her calf muscles and examined their shape. "What's my purpose anymore?"

"Could we brand your face as angular?"
Minny asked.

"Pushing it, really pushing it," I said.

"You could be a character player, a bitter lady
or the smarmy beer wench slinging drinks with a
dragging leg, or a hag in some story in magical technicolor."

Esther groaned and collapsed on the steps.
Minny nudged her and made circles with her hands
over her eyes, snickering.

"Look! Look! There are two birds now!"

"I think when I'm rich, I'll have small space for
four or five birds in my backyard. Some nice cocka-
tiels, or maybe some love birds."

"I would get those Banks' cockatoos. All black
birds. Imagine an aviary full of ravens?"

"Sounds like a nightmare." I said.

"What sort of birds would you have, Pearl?"

"I hate birds. They're filthy. They squawk all
night long. I want to raise Salukis."

"What is a Saluki?"

"It's one of the world's oldest and most elegant
dogs. It's gorgeous—thin, lanky, with luxurious long
hair."

"My home is gonna be a castle filled with exotic creatures and delicious delicacies—fish roe, ur-
chin, Japanese paper." Esther put down her hand
and found a stray cigarette to light. "Who am I kidding? Who's going to hire a gimp?"

"I'm sure some kennel will take you. You can
live with Pearl's Salukis." Minny said.

"Hey..." Esther made moves to stab the hot

end of her cigarette on Minny's arm, all in good fun.

"You don't think it's still possible? For our dreams to come true?" Minny took out a handkerchief bundle containing biscuits, butter, jam, slices of Canadian bacon, and a knife. "I burned the first batch but I think these came out just right, wouldn't you say?"

"You do have a way with baking, Min."

"It's very mathematical, actually. This plus this equals a final product. And if you add wrong, well, your biscuits are bollocks."

"You ever think of opening your own bakery?"

"You think I'm good enough?"

"You could be. You just need a little start-up cash. And a place with style. I bet I could help you there. I have an eye for design. We could draw people in with some bold colors and simple interior. We can call it Babs' Biscuits!"

"Very clever. I say go for it. Maybe we can hit up your beloved Jean Paul Devereaux for a little cash. Give him a few biscuits to taste, maybe look up his assistant and pass them off to her, real sneaky-like, eh?"

"You know, that isn't a bad idea. I could leave them in a little basket with a nice note at his doorstep. Oooo what if we did a delivery treats service like that?"

Minny spread her hands out across the sky and pretended to unfurl a newsprint ad. She put on her best TV mom register. "Too busy to leave the comforts of your Hollywood Hills home? Are you a washed-up recluse with a sweet tooth? Babs' Biscuits to the rescue!"

A funny feeling rumbled in my tummy and up to my chest, contracting my abdomen. A laugh. We were all laughing. We all seemed happy. And then it, Esther, Minny, us, was gone.

The leaves were changing from verdant green to goldenrod. I was the last one left alone at the Bunting house. I was slumped on the porch staring at the flimsy fence that demarcated our land. A plot of wastrel's grass. An unkempt clapboard house. I breathed in dust from the road, found Esther's cigarette butt and lit it up. When I finished that one I walked around foraging for more, lighting them and flicking them away after a single puff. The three of us, my sisters and I, hadn't been apart since the day we were born. We were conjoined to each other, a familial rat king, our demise the result of compacted physicality. Too many mouths breathing in a limited amount of air, a single set of lungs gasping under the weight of three bodies. And three minds stuffed in one body, expanded by oozing out every orifice.

I laid Esther's mink coat down on the steps and fell asleep, waking stiff and confused. In the no-mans-land between awake and asleep I wondered where the furniture had gone, fidgeting with the doorknob and slamming my body against the locked door. *Is this a joke?* I was the joke. My lungs burned and I remembered the cigarettes. On with the show, on with the show, the show must go on, on with the show.

I rinsed my mouth with the spigot, ran my fingers through my hair and applied rouge in the reflection of a window. I changed right there on that front porch for all the world to see into a periwinkle blue day dress. I tucked the note with the address to the casting agency into the breast pocket, walked to the road, and waited for a ride to the bus station. I spent the last of my money on a bus ride from Sky-on-the-Lake, famous for the restorative properties of its waters, to Hollywood. Bus people were my people, private and poor. Bus time was my time, delayed, inefficient, barreling, and sloppy. I boarded the bus after a quick bite, one apple and a cup of coffee. I was high from hunger.

A woman with long features and probing eyes, a woman others might call beautiful but only in the way that money can buy (expensive clothes, treatments, upkeep), motioned for me to take a seat beside her once I'd boarded the bus. I was the lost-looking child. I wanted a seat alone, to stretch my aching hip. But what if I got stuck with someone worse at another stop? A screaming baby, a sweating man?

"You're short," she said, helping me stow my luggage in the compartment overhead.

"Too short?"

She laughed. "No, not too short. Where you headed?"

"Los Angeles."

"What for? Don't tell me you're aiming to be an actress."

"No, someone gave me a free ticket." I fingered Esther's note with the address for the Rose Casting Agency in my pocket.

"That's a nice someone. But Los Angeles isn't really a place you go without a plan. You know anyone there?"

"Sort of."

"Sort of?"

"An old boss."

"A boss? Ain't you a bit young to have had boss already? What'd you used to do, in your youth?"

"I was a dancer, sometimes a singer."

"I can tell that, you have the body. What's your name?"

"Georgia." How easy it was to slip into a new identity through a new name. I was born as an impersonation of two other bodies so the subtle gestures that make a person unique were not lost to me. I could flick my wrist in a way that suggested a privileged upbringing, the upper-crust upper-sides near oceans or waterways. I could bring in a long drawl through the back of my throat to portray a comforting Southern hospitality, or squint my eyes ever so slightly at the corners, giving my face a wrinkled sun-soaked expression—the look of laborers.

"You from the South?"

"Something like that."

The conversation eased as the bus went further along its route and our chat traversed an equally winding terrain of anecdotes, back story, erased or forgotten or misremembered details, and long episodes of silence. Berenice was a chatterbox. I suppose she spent most of her time alone, so that when confronted with a stranger, she was compelled to spill her entire barrel full of beans.

"You should bring me on your interview. I bet I'd bring you good luck. My mom always told me I was blessed since birth. She said I popped right out after a sneeze. I was smiling with a full head of hair. Said I looked just like a china doll." Berenice said as a child she found hundred dollar bills just lying on the side of the road, won every elementary school contest, and every goddamn cereal box sweepstakes giveaway.

"I won so many bikes our backyard looked like a church tag sale. See this watch? I won it." She flashed a gold-linked ladies' Rolex at me. "I'm coming from Vancouver, ever been? I won a trip there in a contest last fall on this show, *Wham Bam Thank You Ma'am*. Heard of it?"

I hadn't.

"Well, I figured I'd leverage my good fortune on the game show circuit, and it worked out. I read an ad for an open call in the Pennysaver one morning and made my way down to the lot the next day. I took the 82 all the way down Fountain. Got my hair blown out the night before and slept sitting up to avoid disturbing my curls. The producers cast me on the spot for Episode 1."

Halfway through the trip we stopped for a break at a roadside. Everyone bought french fries and milkshakes and burgers made on a stovetop grill. I found an abandoned Milky Way and ate it in layers like a squirrel—milk chocolate coating, crunchy nougat, chewy caramel, milk chocolate coating. When it was gone, I was emptier than before I started.

"Want a cup of coffee? My treat." Berenice was touching my shoulder with her palm.

The liquid burned my empty stomach and went straight to my head, causing an overly self-aware mania. I poured a small amount of cream into the cup and licked out the rest from the plastic container with the tip of my tongue.

"Thirty minutes until Los Angeles, folks," the conductor announced.

"So where you staying?"

"Dunno."

"Los Angeles is no place for pretty young girls to go all alone. You can't just show up and expect to find a safe place to lay your head. Say, I have a thought," Berenice said. "My mother would kill me if I let a stranger walk into the belly of the beast without offering some charity. How about I drive you to your appointment tomorrow? But first, why don't you come stay with me? I have an extra room. And I bet I'll rub a little of my luck off on you. My place is a little bit further than Los Angeles, just a bit south. And it's right near the ocean."

No one had ever instilled in us a fear of strangers. We were dumped on strangers by our family, and we dumped ourselves on strangers, bumbling from person to person, mooching, cadging, and sponging. I had no plan in Los Angeles except to show up at Bette or Minny's and freeload. Why not take an offer when it's handed to you? You don't even have to ask and still you'll receive a hand from lady luck.

For the first time I was on my own and could do whatever I pleased. One single day of flying solo and I chose to follow this strange crow.

At the bus depot she pointed at a chic black car

with a white top in the parking lot.

"What kind of car is this, a Chevy?"

"Ford Vedette. Fixed it up myself. Nice, ain't it?"

"Real nice."

Berenice lived in a sleepy port town full of big-armed oil men and amusement parks on the pier. The breeze from the sea soothed the smoggy air. I'd never seen such tall buildings, silver bullets shooting up through the cloud cover. I pushed my body against the edge of a bank and looked up, losing the horizon and all perspective.

"That one belongs to the newspaper dynasty," Berenice said. "And see that one over there? That's the rigger's hall. We can go there after lunch."

"What's that one?" I pointed to a citadel.

"That's city hall."

"It looks like a castle." The city hall in Sandpiper Springs had been a bite-sized converted post office.

"More like a prison. I'm starved, how about I buy you lunch?"

Berenice led me to a small cottage crowded between two giant brick buildings. The windows of the restaurant were four-pane with white panel curtains and a wooden sign over the door: MOLLY's.

"This place has been here since the Gold Rush. It's seen this town go through a lot of different lives, and now, as you see, it's struggling to survive between the vises of financial ventures. It's one of the last vestiges of the good stuff in this town."

We rolled our bags past one, two, three, four

booths and sat in a back booth coated in orange vinyl. The place was packed with dockworkers on their lunch breaks shoveling eggs, pancakes, bacon, and toast and washing it all down with a cocktail of coffee and beer. As we walked past they sized us up, then returned to their concentrated consumption.

Berenice ordered the "World's Fluffiest Johnny Cakes." I went for poached eggs on toast.

"And a small hot coffee, light cream."

"Speak up when you order, honey," the waitress said, taking our menus.

"AND NO BUTTER ON THE TOAST!" I screamed to her through the swinging door to the kitchen.

Arrows shot from all the eyes at the counter.

"Don't worry about her," Berenice said. "She's just playing the role of salty diner waitress."

Our food arrived on hot plates and I ate mine before it had a chance to cool, cutting my knife into the yolk, tinting my toast a gorgeous sunshine yellow. Berenice ate her food at a snail's pace. I left a single bite on my plate to wait for her to catch up. She carved her pancakes into small triangles, pierced three at a time, along with a slice of breakfast sausage, swirled the forkful three times in her maple syrup, and then took a bite, more sucking than chewing her food. She didn't speak while she ate. Once she was finished, I took my last bite of congealed and tepid egg.

"Ready Freddy? Let's settle up and we can head to my place." I didn't bother pretending I would pay when she reached for her pocket book.

Berenice took me to the rigger's hall that night, a repurposed carriage house at the end of the pier. We took shots of liquor I'd never tasted before, liquid that burned my throat just smelling it straight from the bottle. We toasted to my new home, new beginnings, friendships, and to the World's Fluffiest Pancakes. At last call, two longshoreman bought us our final beers.

"You want to know the trick to the game show circuit? Defy the producers. They tell you to stop guessing at a certain money mark, but you watch that little red arrow fly past the 150k line on the circle doohickey, and whoopee! That's where the big bucks come in. You might upset a few here and there, but where there's one show, there's another exactly like it." Her lucky streak continued: a race around the world, two brand-new homes (Santa Fe, New Mexico and Bridgeport, Connecticut), trips to Paris, Rome, and Sao Paolo. A speedboat. Three new cars and a moped, nine television sets, full audio entertainment centers, a shopping spree, and a lifetime supply of Braintree Health Granola. Not to mention all the cash.

"After taxes, it's enough to live a comfy life and support my mother, she lives in the Connecticut house. She keeps asking me when I'm gonna get a real job and I say: when I need one. People get jealous when you're too lucky, though. They start making excuses to touch your arms, your head even, hoping a little of the good karma will rub off on them. Thou shalt not covet they neighbor's jackpot."

"I've been doing it now for fifteen years,

though. I feel it's high time I contributed back to society. All I do is take take take when I don't even ask. So I was up on this trip in Vancouver, figured I'd do a little soul-searching, when I get a phone call. Some producer saw me on the local news (I'm a bit of celebrity in town) and wants to cast me on this new show. I read the script but it's a hooker character. Say, I bet you'd be great for the part!"

"The *fille de joie* with the *joie de vivre*, that's me." I motioned for another shot of the fiery liquor.

The bartender yelled for last call and we left linked arm-in-arm, howling through the streets along with the other riffraff out on a Saturday night. Berenice leaned into my face, all gin and honey breath, and kissed my hand. She sang:

> *Me and you*
> *I think we should*
> *rendezvous*
> *and then we'll*
> *cha cha cha*
> *I'll take it too far*
> *you'll push me*
> *away*
> *but with your a-ok*
> *we'll fly back*
> *to your*
> *place*
> *where I will*
> *seduce*
> *you with my*
> *vatoushes*

a dancer's life for me
and you

I woke up to the smell of the waffle iron, the scent almost enough to overpower the stink of my own rank body. I forgot where I was until my mind caught up with my eyes—a modest second-floor apartment, decorated in periwinkle, the same color of my wrinkled dress. Berenice was in the kitchen, chipper and darting from pan to pan.

"Good morning!" It was the day of Esther's appointment, my appointment. "You look horrible. Here, drink this." She cracked an egg into a cup of coffee and tossed the mug under my nose. "If you're gonna stay with me you're going to have to split the bill. Last night was my treat but from now on it's fifty-fifty on the rent, food, and the fun. Just like last night, yes? I may be lucky, but I'm also smart, and you don't get to be rich by squandering your money on every cute face you meet on a train. Besides, you wouldn't believe what Uncle Sam takes from my winnings in taxes."

I didn't realize I had decided to stay but I was so swept up by the flurry of this woman, and aching from the liquor in muscles I didn't even know I had, that this plan sounded like exactly what I had in mind without my knowing it. I chalked this sudden change of heart up to Berenice not being a morning person.

"We better get a move on if we're going to beat traffic."

"We? You're coming with me?"

"Sure am. You're in need of a manager. No one flies solo in this town. I can play that role. It'll make you look professional, trust me." She held up my blue dress, a bit worse for wear from the night before. "I'll start the car."

I hopped in the car beside Berenice. I did my makeup in the mirror while she drove like an old woman five miles under the speed limit the entire way, pushing me to the doorstep of the Rose Agency at exactly ten am.

The Rose Agency was in a small bungalow in an up-and-coming part of town. Someone had nailed a sign, Cathouse Casting, to the top of the front door.

"I thought it was Rose's?"

"They must be under new ownership. Happens. Happens too often in this town. Come on." Berenice tried to flatten the wrinkles in my dress with her hands and pushed me inside.

I adjusted myself as though I was preparing to step on stage, and limped up the steps to my next role. The parlor of the Cathouse was immaculate and ornate, with high ceilings and a large floor-tile mosaic. A woman met us at the door, an elegant and obese woman dripping in fabrics and costume jewelry. Fake pearl bracelets, a jade clasp, bauble rings and tiers of plastic approximations of diamonds. She saw me eying her heart-shaped yellow diamond.

"These are from a dear aunt, all fake. Cheap is a novelty when you're rich. Did I meet you somewhere, you don't look familiar?" I handed the woman my now-bent appointment card. There really was no point, she had no face to reference.

"No ma'am, one of your agents scouted me up north, in a revue. Bette Bunting's? "

"She's a dancer and a performer. Isn't that right? She's from the south, too. But not country-bumpkin south. She's got this adorable little drawl. Say something, Georgia." Berenice pushed me toward Rose.

"That must have been Richard. He loves those northern women. Well, get out of my way, girl, so I can see her straight." Rose shoved Berenice to the side and placed her hands on my shoulders. She twirled me and felt my haunches with her fat palms. I struggled not to flinch when she squeezed my left leg. She clicked her tongue against her top two teeth.

"Look at you, a real prize pony. You're too young for the juicy parts, though. If Richard wants you, I suppose I'll acquiesce. He's the boss. We do have a small guest role coming up on *Southern Regions*. You'd be playing a teenage prostitute. You okay with that?"

"Would she be nude?" Berenice asked.

"Gosh, no. This is daytime, sweetheart. We write nothing but innuendo. What did you say your name was again?"

"Georgia Starling."

"Ooo, I like it. A little of that southern mystery, a little sass."

Dotted line, here, here, and here. Call time was at four-thirty am.

That night Berenice and I celebrated over a bottle of honey flavored Muscadet and a pile of shrimp cocktail. She was due to ship out to a taping in Acapulco for a new show called *I Do or I Don't*, a matchmaking game. I'd gathered that the real reason she invited me to stay was so she had someone to pay rent while she was gone. For someone who had endless streams of incoming riches (before taxes), she was quite the cheapskate.

"When we're done with the pictures, let's open our own bar." Berenice had a nasty way of eating shrimp. She shoved the whole creature in her mouth and chewed the shell off with her lips closed. She then sucked the remains out like a magician pulling the endless scarf trick.

"Beer and wine only?"

"And a few snacks, something easy."

"Like cheese sandwiches?"

"Or bowls of peanuts."

It was hot and beads of water ran down the two tall glasses Berenice had poured. Beads of sweat gathered in my bra, my armpits, my fingertips. I watched the beads on Berenice's face turn to shimmering beads, the kind that make up a child's necklace. I went to bed early for beauty rest and woke long before the sun was set to rise. I went to makeup to get my face done up professionally and then was fitted for my costume.

"Sweetie, you're tiny. I wish I had those hips. The waif look is very in this year. But you don't fit in any of our clothes!" The costumer pinned my shirt at my back and clipped the belt of my pants.

"You'll be sitting in this scene, so as long as you don't make any sudden movements, no one will notice."

More sweat dripping from my costar's face, rolling down his shirt collar and lingering in the folds of flesh that gathered below his chin. I wondered why Rose had cast this one, she seemed to have better taste. Her business was good, wasn't it? This man wasn't even wearing a good suit. I examined my own costume, rough-shod and itchy polyester that sagged at the knees. The makeup girl had told me I had eczema, which I scratched at with my nails, rubbing a bit of the cat-eye she'd drawn on my lids off with my greasy finger. She'd told me that if it wasn't for the dry patches, I could have been a beauty queen in another life.

My costar was Elvis Kresge, a character actor with a few walk-on roles to his name. We chatted while the set designers put the final touches on the props in the room.

"You hear of Kamille Kresge? The real estate agent? She's the best and most successful real estate agent in town. If you ever need a room, you let me know and I'll give you her number." Elvis and Kamille had met while he was filling up his tank of gas at the station where she worked a night shift while she was taking real estate classes. He'd stayed with her until closing, then walked her home and never left.

We were sitting on a peach colored bed, in Madam A's, the fake whorehouse in *Southern Regions*. I was playing the role of Peachy Keen, the young-in-age but old-at-heart lady of the night. He was telling me about his wife's obsession with commemorative figurines and stroking my hair.

"Look bored, Georgia. You're flat-out bored with this man," the director said, slumped over in his chair. I recognized his name from somewhere. Something French, Devereaux. This was going to be easy.

"Peachy, sweet, sweet Peachy. How you been? You missed me? You haven't aged a bit. Still fresh as a daisy spring chicken. How old are you now? Seventeen? Eighteen? Can't be seventeen, that'd be unlawful. Must be eighteen, nineteen, heck maybe twenty!"

"Twenty, Mr. B. My birthday was just last June."

"Twenty, hoo wee, and look at you. You don't look a day over sixteen. Peach, where you been? Haven't seen you around in a while."

"I been out tryna to get straight."

"Trying to get straight? What for? Seems to me you got a right good life here. You got a place to live, and a man like me to love ya."

"This life just ain't Christian. I was raised Born Again, you know. When I was five I kneeled and accepted Jesus into my heart as my lord and savior. And somehow, somewhere, along the line I got greedy and the devil tempted me off my path. But I want to get back on that path."

The storyline was ridiculous and the writing was slack. My character was trying to break out of the working girl life and back into a life of a good Christian woman. I couldn't tell if Peach was kidding or not, just to get rid of this man in front of her. And if she was serious, where was her story leading?

Was I some little match girl to be pitied?

"Don't tell me you've been brainwashed by all that mumbo jumbo from the women who hole up outside a' the Woolworth's?"

"It was the Army Navy and they gave me some nice pieces of literature to peruse." *Peruse*? Would a sixteen-year-old prostitute use the word *peruse*?

"What am I going to do without you?"

"Oh you can't tell no one, Mr. B. But I'm not sure how long this place is gonna last. There are ... people watching. If you know what I mean."

"You mean the Feds?"

"The Feds? Really? Isn't that a bit dramatic? Maybe the LAPD, but they'd probably be more inclined to keep this place around for their own pleasure, don't you think?" I threw my script down and implored the director for some logic.

"Just read the lines, sweetheart."

"Fine." I adjusted myself. "All I know is this one guy came around asking for Lady A and no one asks for Lady A directly. He was practically flashing his badge. At first I thought, *oh boy here we go, another blue looking to blackmail us for a little hush-hush action*. But then he never came back and none of the other girls said they saw him neither."

Elvis mocked dismay at his wristwatch.

"Would you look at the time? I'm running late. Told my wife I'd cook for her tonight. Imagine that? Me, cook! I hope she likes sandwiches. Heh, heh. All right little lady." He patted me on the knee twice. "I'll be seeing you, good luck with Jesus and all that."

The round blueberry of a man maneuvered into a boxy blazer and angled his way off set. We ended the scene with me on my knees praying silently. I improvised an impression of innocence to draw out during last looks.

My episode aired on March 10 at two PM on channel 4, KWXYQ. Peachy Keen was an instant hit with audiences and I was signed on for a full two seasons of this ridiculous show. I didn't have the imagination to see myself as anything other than a winking star.

EAT YOUR HEART OUT

It's not so difficult to find out things in Hollywood. The grapevine is wide and echoing. The three of us may have gone our separate ways but one never disconnects. Minny had taken her chances and ran after Bette, riding her coattails all the way to Hollywood. Turns out, all those secret trips were Bette's networking meetings with TV executives. I heard she was working on one big threat to one big executive regarding a forty-plus-year affair exposé. To keep her quiet, he offered her a slot on a late-night show, plus market shares. She knew we didn't stand a chance as a package deal but as a solo act, she could finally, perhaps, run a star show. Nothing remained secret in this business and this all became flash-in-the-pan news and then the storyline disappeared.

She wasn't thrilled with her slot—a late-night talk show? And the producers always booked washed-up celebrities. Ratings weren't terrible, though. The viewers up late enough were certainly intrigued by the absurdity of it all. Or they were too drunk from a night out to notice they weren't intrigued. And Bette was still a looker in her waning days. She was tall and strong with mounds of wavy hair, a muscular sort of graceful. She smelled strongly of peonies and it was rumored that she bathed in flower petals. The show got the top rating for the time slot and drew in cult, some would say B-grade, celebrities. She put Minny on her assistant crew, and sometimes she'd appear in the show's "Blast From the Past" nostalgia bit—a throwback dream sequence of bygone and hackneyed sketches.

When the executives announced they wanted to produce a spin-off of Bette's variety show comboed with a flailing kid's show from my youth, she pegged my sister to star as the naive philosopher with our former beloved puppet co-stars: Dust Bunny the well-meaning but dull piece of bedside lint, and Sweet Tooth, the frantic and failed (but passionate) pastry chef.

"It's a comedic cooking show for mothers. We're slating it for that pre-dinner slump."

The show was imagined as a short-term no-fail showcase for endorsements: the latest frozen, microwavable, boxed, packaged, convenience food for the busy mom. To the surprise of everyone, myself included, the puppets were a hit for two seasons. The time slot hit the spot for stay-at-home moms who waited until the last minute to plan dinner and still had kids at home who needed entertaining. The show was both a chance for bored moms and bored kids to bond over a combination of philosophical musings and slapstick cooking disasters. I'd watch it from time to time if I had a moment to spare between bookings, or on the tiny unit while I did my face in my dressing room. The jokes sometimes went over the little ones' heads and yet hit them right on the noses.

Each episode started the same way. The format hadn't changed since I used to watch the program as a kid, but the scripts were updated for a more modern audience. *Sweet Tooth's Bakestravaganza Baking and Cooking Show and Sometimes Talk Show Show!* zipped across the screen in garish colors. This faded into a young woman, now played by Minny (I couldn't for the life of me remember who played this role when I was a kid), with grey hair cut short, wearing very small round glasses, a wide shouldered black angora sweater and coral trousers, sitting at the kitchen counter with a typewriter, facing the screen. As always, to her left was Sweet Tooth, even more frazzled now, the single long spiked rock candy tooth hanging from her drooling mouth to her chest. To her right sat the Dust Bunny, now a cross between a piece of bellybutton lint and a tumbleweed. The show was now in color. I was shocked to see that Sweet Tooth was ultramarine, her hair not blond, but a garish orange.

The first episode Minny wrote on was "Meringues." I will say I felt a bit of a thrill seeing the Starling name in the scrolling byline. Sweet Tooth sat looking forlorn at the kitchen island. She was surrounded by egg cartons. She cracked eggs absent-mindedly into a large metal bowl. Dust Bunny looked over the Minny's shoulder as she stared blankly at the typewriter. A peppy offstage voice announced: "Sweet Tooth's Bakestravaganza Baking and Cooking Show and Sometimes Talk Show Show,

Channel 4. Today's guest: a slice of bacon! And as always, music accompaniment by Bobbi Egg-White and The Gum Wads. Take it away, Bobbi!" The music used to be a gentle and mostly background noise, but now it was loud and alarming, in the style the kids enjoyed these days. Bobbi Egg-White looked like death with all his tendons revealed and fraying. The camera zoomed in on Sweet Tooth.

"397. 398. 399. 400. Shoot! I forgot to separate the yolks." Sweet Tooth pulled out a large ladle and began to scoop out eggs and throw the goop on the floor and table.

"The secret to stiff meringue is having absolutely zero nilch nada none nein yolk."

"What are you making, Sweet Tooth?" Minny leaned over her bowl to peer at the contents—nothing but a goop of egg whites.

"Lemon meringue pie! With the stiffest peaks of meringue, the jelliest of lemon filling, and, of course an extra flaky, extra buttery crust."

"Scrumptious! I can't wait to try a slice."

"Should only take eight more hours!"

"What? Really? But I'm starved!"

"The secret to baking is patience!"

"You know, pie was invented by the Egyptians." Dust Bunny stepped in, he was now wearing glasses with a broken frame and cracked lenses.

"That can't possibly be true." Minny removed Dust Bunny's glasses and peered through the lenses. She placed them with care back on Dust Bunny's face.

"But it is! You see, the Egyptians were sick of

matzo after the Jews left, so they made these round pans, because round is the easiest shape you can make, you see, and they tried to bake the matzo in the round pans. But it just crumbled in the sun. So they figured out if they added animal fat...."

"That's called lard!" Sweet Tooth interrupted. She waved her spatula and sent half-beaten egg whites across the kitchen. The gloved hands appeared and dabbed at the mess with a towel.

"Thank you, Sweet Tooth." Dust Bunny cleaned his glasses with a towel handed to him by one of the gloves. "The Jewish people figured out if they added lard that the matzo wouldn't break and it would form this little... this solid form and that it also tasted delicious! Or at least, it tasted edible. And so they thought, 'hm, well if there are no more cracks, we can add all the things that are not quite liquid and not quite solid that we've been making and they won't leak through!' So they did just that and set it in the sun and there you have it. Et voilà! There was the first pie."

"Oh what a great story! I do love pie! Butter and sugared fruit and sometimes meringue! Or à la mode. That means With Ice Cream," Sweet Tooth said.

"That is the looniest tall tale I've ever heard. I'm pretty sure that famous chef, that woman, what's her name? She invented the pie," Minny's character said.

"Who?" Dust Bunny was still polishing his glasses. They now cast a blinding glare toward the camera. He pointed them at an angle from the sun beating through the window and fried an egg on the countertop.

"I can't remember her name. You know the one, though, I'm sure of it. The big lady? With the apron? She had very tall hair. I think she made her name in tea cakes."

"Oh! Tea cakes! What a great idea for next week's episode! We can have a tea party. I'll make scones and biscuits!"

"You know, the art of the tea ceremony is lost on Americans. It's a shame, in my opinion." Dust Bunny was now inspecting the fine china with his glasses. His clumsy hands dropped each precious cup one after the other to the floor.

"Where was I...oh yes! 401, 402, 403..." Sweet Tooth cracked countless more eggs. She was surrounded by their shells. A baby dinosaur emerged from one shell and one of the gloved hands swatted it back down.

"How much meringue are you making?!"

"Just a few more... 404, and 405! Done! Now we get out our whisks and add the sugar!" Sweet Tooth pulled out a whisk but it wasn't large enough to get the job ahead done. She ducked down, making a ruckus looking for a better tool in her kitchen island. Meanwhile Dust Bunny's square mouth pursed inward to his face, disappearing altogether. He had been leaning his elbows in egg yolk.

"Yuck! Egg yolk everywhere! Disgusting!"

"Oh! Shall we fry them up into an omelet? No use wasting them, eh?" A thought bubble cartoon of a fluffy omelet appeared above Minny's head. I wondered why my sister didn't dye her hair, grey really didn't suit her coloring.

"This should do the trick!" Sweet Tooth emerged from under the counter with a unicycle in her hands, holding it aloft like a prized trophy. She struggled with the weight and four gloves appeared to prop the wheel up.

"Think of all the enjoyable things made with egg yolks! Custard! Soufflé! That pasta sauce made with egg yolk!" More thought bubbles appeared above Minny's head. Red hearts appeared on the lenses of Dust Bunny's glasses.

"You know, the egg yolk came before the egg, which came after the chicken," Dust Bunny said.

"Hm, the bike won't fit."

"I believe they showed up at the same time." Minny clutched her stomach and eyed all the food, drooling. A low grumble crescendoed into a deafening noise. Dust Bunny covered his ears and fainted. Meanwhile, Sweet Tooth dragged a large metal tub with her back into the kitchen. She picked up the bowl of egg whites and dumped them in the larger tub with a flop. Then she placed the unicycle in the tub and hoisted herself on the unicycle in the tub and rode around in circles, her knobby knees raising up to her chin in a piston-like motion.

"The secret to meringue is to beat the egg whites very hard!"

"I thought the secret was no egg yolk?"

"Can one of you do me a favor and hand me that bag of sugar?" Dust Bunny threw Sweet Tooth a sack of sugar, but one of the gloves caught it for her.

Sweet Tooth continued to ride the unicycle while the hand dumped sugar into the tub.

"The secret to meringue is to add the sugar very slowly."

"But you just said…"

"Oh! We're getting there! We're getting there! See how soft peaks are forming?"

"Oh! Yes, just like Mt. Kilimanjaro!" Dust Bunny took a peek into the tub. Minny was gathering yolks in her hands and placing them in the now-empty mixing bowl.

"The Swiss Alps! Oh the Swiss do know how to make their sweets! Chocolates and jellies and those little chocolates with white sprinkles!"

Minny snuck a pat of butter into a skillet on the stove.

"Non-pareils," she said over her shoulder while fussing with the pilot light on the stove.

"Pardon?"

"Non-pareils. That's what those candies are called. It translates as, something like "dissimilar," in French."

"How peculiar!"

"I know why!" Sweet Tooth paused from her cycling and tottered side to side. "Because one part is black and the other white! But it's all the same to me: delish!"

"They were my mother's favorite candy. She'd eat a whole box in one sitting."

"Who wouldn't?" Sweet Tooth returned to her hectic unicycle beating.

"I tried to like them because my mom did, but

they weren't my favorite."

"Ooo wooooo! Look at these peaks!" The meringue peaks had grown quite large—they projected up to the ceiling and filled the room.

I bet you could ski off these things!"

"Great idea, Dust Bunny!" Sweet Tooth abandoned her unicycle and bolted off stage. A stagehand raced after her on all floors, trying avoid to the camera.

Meanwhile, Minny gently beat the eggs with a fork and added a bit of water. She tested the temperature of the skillet by placing her hand over the top. She gave a look of satisfaction to the camera—a single raised eyebrow and a smirk, amateur— and added the eggs to the pan. They sizzled.

"My mother used milk in her eggs. I never knew why. I like to taste the eggs. So, I use water. You only need a bit, anyway."

Sweet Tooth reappeared in full ski gear and downhill skis. She pulled ski goggles over her face and mounted the meringue peaks.

"Now that the meringue is done, we can add it to the pie!" She shouted from the mountaintop. "I made the crust last night. The secret to a good crust is letting the butter get cold! And I made the filling this morning, so it could congeal."

"That's how it comes together! Contrast keeps things interesting! Contrast and conflict and climax are crucial to any story." Minny flipped the omelet over onto a plate and slid it back in the pan to cook the other side. She waited a few moments then repeated the process, this time leaving the eggs on the plate and turning off the stove. She found a fork and knife and sat on a stool at the kitchen island, taking a hearty bite.

"I thought we were talking about baking."

"Now we're ready to add the meringue to the pie." Sweet Tooth had taken one of her skis to pile the white peaks onto the pie, burying it.

"It's a metaphor, Dust Bunny."

"Now we bake the pie! I already preheated the oven to 350°. So, stick the pie in the oven on a low rack for an hour and wait wait wait! Oh waiting is the worst part of baking!"

A prop boy entered the stage holding a massive egg timer. He spun the hands to the very end and let it begin. The Gum Wads played along to the tick tick tick. The camera cut to the three of them aging: hair getting long and more grey, wrinkles appearing, Dust Bunny disappearing, Sweet Tooth shriveling, Minny becoming hunched.

"This is taking too long!" Sweet Tooth turned the egg timer ahead several turns until it dinged. They remained old and all their movements were now slowed down. "Done! Make sure to remove the pie with insulated oven mitts." She used her ski gloves to remove the pie. It emerged with a towering meringue. Her arm pulled back to take aim at Minny's face, and then at Dust Bunny.

"Which of you wants it?"

Dust Bunny and Minny pointed at one another and ducked behind the counter. A little white flag raised.

"I'm kidding! We have to let it cool anyway so it gets those little sugar dew drops. We love those sugar dew drops, don't we?" Sweet Tooth was cooing and nuzzling close to the pie. "It shouldn't be long. But for now, I'm off to the lodge. I'll be back by next week when we will work on those Swiss goodies. Au revoir sweeties!"

"I want to go! Wait for me!" Dust Bunny followed her off stage, rolling himself like desert chaparral across the floor.

Minny leaned back and patted her now ample tummy, happy and full from the eggs. She swiped a finger in the meringue.

"Mm. Delicious."

The title, once again, shot across the screen: *Sweet Tooth's Bakestravanza Baking and Cooking Show and Sometimes Talk Show Show*. The fireman puppeteer entered the set and sprayed a fire extinguisher, adding to the sugar peaks until the entire screen filled with white and the episode concluded in this inverse fade out.

Some people said Minny was at the height of her career when the show was cancelled and was looped into Bette's talk show as a shorter skit. The producers claimed they wanted to make airspace for a new soap about a family of confederate ghosts living in New Orleans with scads of scandals and secrets. I'm sure all Minny got was a goodbye cake from the freezer aisle and a mediocre severance check. What was so special about family secrets? Every family has secrets. But people wanted more scripted fiction. Gotta keep up with the times, stay current, fresh, modern. Fake it til you make it.

She returned to Bette's office begging for another job. Bette understood that we had to take care of each other in this business so she gave Minny a job writing on her show, with the caveat that she'd never appear in front of camera again. Minny took the deal.

Bette's talk show, *The Witching Watching Hour*, was on a soundstage on a lot surrounded by other sound stages and lots surrounded by a cemetery for the rich and famous. The writers built this unique and natural setting into the show as a Bette's *This is Your Afterlife!* skit. Guests were blindfolded and carted from the set to the graveyard where they would walk and talk about bygone stars. Then the guest would reach their own prop grave, and someone gleaned from their past would tell the story of their life. Her ratings were taking a nosedive. Viewers were only interested in formulaic sitcoms or game show shenanigans. Bette's producers made it clear that if her ratings didn't improve by May sweeps, her show was doomed to the cutting room floor. It would be her in the graveyard soon enough, if things didn't improve.

It was Minny's idea, I'm certain of it, to find me and Esther. I was on that hit soap now, *Southern Regions*. I had a bit of a following. I can hear her squidgy voice now, 'What if we did a reunion on your set? Think of it: three former beauties, stage stars of yore, reunited for the first time right here on your set! We could even get the other girls from the revue, if we can find them.'

It was a bit devious, even for me. But I couldn't blame them, that's the nature of television. We all survive on ads, major product tie-ins built around nostalgia—you know, tugging at the oldsters' heart strings.

The wicked girl had a good idea for once and Bette liked it. So did the producers. Reaching me would be no problem, I had an agent now and I still loved being in front of a camera. I'd already booked fourteen commercials that aired during my own soap. I was the face of daytime scripted television. Minny called my agent who arranged a time to meet. We met at hot new luau themed restaurant. We both ordered the special: lime fish with coconut cream and two extra-large Mai Tais.

"You have to be okay with surprises, Pearl," she said. "It's part of the deal."

"Fine, fine. I can play the bombshelled bombshell." I motioned for the check and signed the contract. I hadn't heard from my sister, either of them, in god knows how long. So when Esther asked me to appear on the show she was writing on for Bette, I thought, why not? What's a few hours for family? And it was perfectly timed with my soap's new season. Esther would take a bit more finagling. She was out of the limelight. She lived where the flow of communication was cut off at the throat, back in the desert of Sandpiper Springs.

Our old neighbor Maggie had once written me a fan letter. She apparently was a real admirer of me and my show. In her PS she told me she found out Esther had resurrected the old orange trailer. The thing was still intact and needed only a bit of de-cob-webbing. It was fully furnished, too, if not rusty and mildewed. Esther, apparently, was working days at The Homewood, a sort of health spa near the hot springs. I saw an ad for it once in the Pennysaver. *BEWARE OF UNTRAINED RITUALS.* It read. *Full Moon in Cancer Meditation at the Homewood Sandpiper Meditation and Wellness Center). We have the cures for what ails you.* It was a mere thirty miles southwest of Sandpiper Springs. It all sounded like a bunch of hooey to me. But I can't imagine Esther's revue money lasted more than a few months and she could only live so long on the goodwill of the landlord. My sister was a smart cookie, she knew she lost her edge in the fall and there was no getting it back now, she knew that things moved on without you at high speed in this business.

The Homewood Sandpiper was once a city building, a corinthian-columned Monticello of a lake house for the wayward. There was a wraparound porch, picture windows on all sides, well-manicured grounds (including a labyrinth for contemplative wandering). Our dad brought us there once when it was a hall of records, for some sort of paperwork or lien or some such. Through the front double doors marble extended out toward visitors like white frozen waves, leading up to the receptionist's desk. Upon registration, guests had two options: a room full of maps with a view of the lake or a room full of genealogy reports with a view of the mountains. The rooms were also marbled and white, minimally furnished with reading chairs and indoor ferns. I specifically recall that there were no mirrors anywhere on the premises.

This is where Minny rung Esther and delivered the news that would get her to Hollywood—that the Cuckoo had passed and arranged her own funeral—an elaborate and expensive (no doubt) burial at a coveted resting place for deceased Hollywood elite. She would rest for all eternity amid the corpses of her imagined peers.

"It'll be easy, Esther. All you have to do is join us at the private viewing next week, at the Cemetery of the Eternal," Minny said. Ever the dutiful daughter, Esther packed her things, a single suitcase full of her old costumes and wigs.

On the day my interview with Bette was to air I sat in the green room practicing quippy answers to anticipated questions—*No, I really do prefer being on the other side of the camera. It's much easier on my diet! Or lack thereof! Am I seeing anyone? I'm seeing lots of anyones, darling.* I was getting my eyes painted the color of bruised apples and listening to the show backstage.

The stage set for *The Witching Watching Hour with Bette Bunting* looked like an explosion in a frosting factory. The walls from floor to ceiling were painted a sickening cotton-candy pink. Bette and her guests sat on a crisp white leather couch, or on the floor on a white shag rug. She always wore a starched white pantsuit and dyed her graying hair ultra-platinum every week, to ensure she matched her surroundings. She feathered it in the latest style, but didn't want to appear as though she were trying too hard.

"Keep it natural," she'd snap at the hair-and-makeup girl as she applied can after can of hairspray.

"A successful career woman such as myself shouldn't look as though she has time to spend on looking good." She was tan (fake) and thin (real).

A new artist's work was featured in the backdrop every week. Tonight, a reflective St. Rita, patron saint of family feuds, glimmered behind Bette's couch.

The show opened with an off-screen voice:

> *Stand still, you ever-moving spheres of*
> *heaven,*
> *That time may cease, and midnight*
> *never come.*

But in the meantime, it's Show-Time for everyone's favorite late night talk show, The Witching Watching Hour with Bette Bunting. *Tonight's guest stars are: ten-year-old wunderkind Little Toni; former stage-star and vedette turned star of the daytime soap scene, Georgia, formerly Pearl, Starling; and musical guest The Hopscotch Willies. And of course, as always, our house band Vinny Vincenzo and the Twilight Orchestra, everyone's favorite sidekick puppets: Sweet Tooth and Dust Bunny, and your host, the gorgeous, the incomparable, the incorrigible, the verrrrrrrrrrrry delightful: Bette Bunting!*

Lights would spot on Bette, looking fabulous in her tailored tux, sitting in a very easy pose on her couch. Her costars, Sweet Tooth and Dust Bunny sat in tiny armchairs holding tiny mugs of cocoa. The content of the show toed the line between smut and decent humor. Together, the trio would hash out the news, speak in puns and idioms, and lead the audience into the show.

"Hi Sweet Tooth."

"Hi Bette!"

"Hi Dust Bunny."

"Hi Bette!"

"Say, Sweet Tooth, have you seen the new Marilyn Monroe?"

"Oh yes, vavavavooooom!"

Offstage, an assistant rips a sound effect of a hot rod engine.

"She's muy talented, no?"

"Is that what they're calling it these days? We can thank her mother for her talents, then!"

"So, Sweet Tooth, what have you been working on?"

"I'm so glad you asked, Bette. I'm currently perfecting my apple turnover recipe. Just in time for Thanksgiving!"

"But Sweet Tooth, it's May!"

"It's a slow process."

Bette pauses for audience laughter. She rolls her eyes in the direction of the audience as if to say *You see what I'm working with here?*

"Well, it's not slow tonight! We have a very zippy show for you all. I'm so excited for our guests tonight, you two. First up, we have Little Toni here to sing us an operatic solo from *La Traviata*."

"Will she sing us a drinking song? I do love those. Yo ho ho, the Irish life for me!"

"That's not a very nice thing to say, that's a stereotype Sweet Tooth."

"But I think drinking is quite nice."

"I think you'll be even more thrilled for our second guest. Famously flexible star of the stage turned soap opera lioness, my former protégé Pearl Starling!"

"Now I could really use some of that Irish influence."

"And finally, we have The Hopscotch Willies, all the way from Tijuana Mexico, to serenade us into the night."

"Muy caliente!"

"But before we start, I want to say that tonight we learned of the passing of one of our guests' mothers. Mrs. Georgia 'Cuckoo' Starling, aged seventy-four, passed away soundly in her sleep last night. Our heartfelt condolences go out to my guest, Pearl Starling. But like a true performer, and in the spirit of her free bird mama, Ms. Starling has agreed to go on with the show! That's the chutzpah I like to see in this business. Besides, there's no better medicine than laughter, wouldn't you agree?"

"Hear, hear!"

"Hear, hear!" Dust Bunny and Sweet Tooth cheered with their hot chocolate. A bit spilled over the sides. Sweet Tooth licked both her mug and Dust Bunny's mug.

"Okay then, on with the show! As always, our house band Vinny Vincenzo and the Twilight Orchestra will lead us there. Take it away, Vinny!"

The orchestra faded to a safe snare introduction to Little Toni, an obese girl of ten or so made up to look like a Russian nesting doll. Or perhaps this was her real look—one can hope. She was covered in cloaks and scarves, a babushka slung around her head and clipped at her fat little neck. She cleared her throat and sang an operatic aria, a requiem. She mocked her own death, wheezing and coughing and clutching her chest. Amateur.

Morir si giovane!
To die so young!

When her song was over, Bette beckoned Little Toni to her talking couch.

"Wasn't that wonderful? You, young lady, are going to be famous. You have some talent. Where did you learn to sing like that?"

"I practiced in my bathroom every morning."

Awww, How precious. Isn't she adorable? Isn't she divine? Have you ever seen anything that darling?

"Of course you did, and I can tell! And what do you want to be when you grow up?"

"The President of the United States of America."

"Well, a girl with ambition to boot! Thank you, Little Toni. Keep it up and I'm sure you'll be giving us all a run for our money one day. Next up, we have Pearl Starling, star of *Southern Regions*. Word of warning: we have our censors on hand, but it may get steamy in here, because Ms. Starling is one hot ticket. So maybe send those kiddies off for a midnight snack for a few moments—I'd suggest a Blammo double-dipped butterscotch bar or a glass of McFetridge white chocolate chocolate milk. But before we meet our next guest, a brief word from our sponsor."

They cut to a commercial for some new chocolate drink, and Bette ran to my makeup room.

"Sorry about your mom, should I keep doing your bronzer?" The makeup girl asked. I was stunned. I had learned of my mother's death from the backstage teleprompter.

"Pearl—should I be calling you Georgia now?— dear, you look ravishing. You're aging so well. Sorry about your Mom." Bette took a lock of my hair and curled it around her ring finger.

"You couldn't have told me in private backstage, Bette?"

"You mean you didn't know? I had no idea, I thought I was rehashing old news to you, I surely thought you'd have known. I was just setting the stage for our audience. I figured we could talk about moving through grief through art."

"No Bette. It's the first time I'd heard of it." I was still a ravenous consumer of the dailies, but I couldn't have expected to find the obit for a two-bit lounge singer in whatever backwater town the Cuckoo had finally blown into.

"Do you want to go on? Please say you do. We could make history here, my darling. You could do an homage. That'll really get 'em, play the dead mother card."

From a business perspective, I couldn't disagree. The timing was horrible, my mother was selfish even with her death. The Cuckoo dropped us off as babies, left us at the threshold of womanhood. She taught us to follow our guts and go where there would be rewards.

"Finish my face," I told the makeup girl.

Bette returned to her set, adjusted herself, her hair, and refreshed her beverage. She was poised at an erect forty-five degree angle to announce my arrival.

"Our next guest is a star of both stage and screen, and a dear friend. We've worked together since she was not much older than Little Toni. At age—what was it dear, thirteen? Sweet sixteen?—she joined my revue, and became one of our most talented stars, alongside her two identical sisters, Esther and Minny. Triple beauts. Unfortunately, the Starling Sisters triplet act was short-lived, but tonight we're lucky enough to have Ms. Georgia, formerly Pearl, Starling, who once had a way with her hips and now has a way with her lips as the lead in the hit daytime soap, *Southern Regions*. Ladies and gentlemen, Ms. Georgia Starling!"

I had picked a fuzzy orange angora sweater and slim-cut iridescent capris. My nails were manicured, my hair was long and natural, but the makeup girl had practically ruined my look with her heavy hand. At first, Bette and I chatted about the show, my character's latest plot twist—I was a Russian spy—and what viewers could expect next season. But then the Twilight Orchestra interrupted my speech with the chords of Chopin's funeral march.

"Uh oh. You know what that means folks. It's time for *This Is Your Afterlife!* Ms. Starling, are you ready to learn the fate you'd otherwise never know?"

"No, but I suppose I'll have to be." I'd watched Bette's shows for ages now and was familiar with all her corny gags. My agent said appearing on this silly show would make me appear versatile, or did she use the word "personable"?

Bette took out a long piece of fabric and a slip of folded paper. "Fantastic. Tonight's honorary blindfolder is the guest in seat number 162. Will the guest in seat number 162 please come to the stage and blindfold Ms. Starling?"

A tiny girl in pigtails skipped down the aisles and snatched the blindfold from Bette's hand. She placed the fabric, with much flourish, across my eyes, and tied it firm against my head.

"What's your name, honey?"

"Lily Robinson from Potentia."

"Thank you, Lily Robinson from Potentia. Now, tonight on *This is Your Afterlife!*, you, Georgia Starling, will meet your identical sisters for the first time in five years. Big family secrets will be revealed, and there may be a surprise guest or two. But first, a word from our sponsor."

On a Saturday at noon, a drizzling day, a slow day, a woman in a tie-neck blouse enters an Italian deli-style shop. Bromide ding of door's bell. She is shaped like a squeezed grape, the blood rushed to her face. Her hair is tucked neatly under a stiff box hat. Long immaculate gloves. Paulie, the proprietor, remembering his mom (thought bubble flashback of her pulling elbow-length gloves up each arm before going out with his father to the club or the Elk Lodge). Paulie checks his watch as if it could read the decade. (Sees decade, rubs eyes in disbelief, watch now reads 12:04 pm.) Still Saturday. Still rain-

ing. Still six more hours to close (extended weekend schedule).

The woman speaks:

"I saw your sign for a new ravioli. Could you tell me more about that?"

"You must mean the gnocchi, ma'am. And I apologize, but that isn't new. Just haven't gotten around to taking that thing down. It's a very popular item, though. I'd recommended a cream-based sauce to accompany."

"Gnocchi? But is that like ravioli?"

"No ma'am. It's a pasta dumpling made with potato."

"Oh! Like a knish! How delightful. How much would you recommend for a dinner party of twelve?"

"Hard to say ... will there be appetizers? Is it a hardy crowd? Or delicate eaters?"

"I'm not sure. I've never thrown a dinner party before. What would you recommend for appetizers?" The woman fidgets, examining a box of squid ink linguine.

Paulie sizes the woman up. Stockings. Closed toe pumps. Proper, a real lady. Not like those messes of girls that stumble in here after day drinking in the park, asking for diet soda, fancy water, or fawning over stale wedding cookies.

"I would recommend a nice cured meat. Soppressata, perhaps."

"Meat! Yes, of course! We'll need meat."

Did sparks fly from her spit in this outburst? Paulie begins to slice a hock.

*The woman fills her basket with Italian delica-
cies, holding each item close to her face in wonder-
ment. Olive oil! Long thin breadsticks. Parmigiano.*

"Being exotic is très chic. No one can get away
with presenting a typical casserole these days. No
more tuna noodle. No more canned tomato soup.
I'm shocked your store is so well-stocked, what with
the rations."

Rations? Paulie wonders.

*The woman hums "Bali Ha'i," from South
Pacific.*

"My mother loved that musical."

*The woman pauses. Her mouth twitches.
Loved? Past tense?*

"Loved? A recent death?"

"No, ma'am. She passed twenty years ago this
November."

She twitches.

"But that's impossible. South Pacific is the
movie of the year!"

*Paulie pauses his slicing. This woman reminds
him of someone. Ms. Danby, the mother of one of
his mother's kindergartners. A clueless woman with
a rich husband. German descent, he thought. On
Halloween she gave out pennies. When he visited her
house, she served red hard candies in a blue glass jar.
"I just love the contrast," she said. No, it wasn't Ms.
Danby. It was, no, it couldn't be...*

"Hello dear," his mother says. "I'm so glad
you'll be joining us for dinner."

*Cut to close up of a woman's gloved hand
and another hand extending from a butcher's sleeve*

holding a jar of tomato sauce. Cue voiceover.

Paulie's Handmade Pasta and Pasta Sauce— for when you're craving a mother's touch, but she's just out of reach.

THIS IS YOUR AFTERLIFE

Bette leaned back in the seat of the golf cart. She pressed her thumb and forefinger to the bridge of her nose.

"What a flop. This show makes me want to retch sometimes, you know that? If we don't get renewed, I'm going to retire. I'll move to some cabin in the Hills. Maybe I'll try my hand at writing romance novels."

Bette was wrong: her next life would be spent in the Keys, were she'd pick up a gig as the host on a gameshow for retirees called *Snowbirds*. At night she would chip away at her romance novel, a bawdy story about a vampire with a heart of gold whose appetite is activated via remote control. Whoever held the remote, held the power. She'd get stuck on a chapter in which the remote falls into the hands of an eleven-year-old boy with leukemia and a few bones to pick.

"For now, they want a show and my job is to give them what they want." As the scripts got more and more melodramatic, nothing satiated unless it was a gruesome death followed by an unbelievable resurrection, or mistaken identities, or evil doppelgängers. The proximity to the sinister amplified the beauty of the audience's lives off-screen.

"Here we are," Bette said, sweeping her arm toward the graveyard, to a dummy tomb with STARLING in bas-relief at the top of the vault door. A boyish man named Steve, the show's line producer, stood waiting for us with a clipboard and an ear mic. I anticipated some antic and had stayed up late rehearsing "surprise" and "warm-hearted but off-put." How to Appear Shocked and Then Up For Anything. Spontaneity Can Be Fun! But no amount of training could have prepared me for the gravestone with my name on it when Steve removed my blindfold in front of a live audience. *Here Lies Georgia née Pearl Starling. Light of Stage and Screen. Beloved Sister (twice-over) and Daughter.* My "oh, you scoundrel" look twitched and short-circuited.

"What's this, Bette?" The words came out without delineation thanks to my clenched jaw.

"Pearl, I mean Georgia, Starling,

This

Is

Your

Afterlife!

(recorded applause)

Now is the time to confess and be forgiven. Only then can you pass to the next round, the Heav-

en's Gate, *sponsored by McFetridge Powdered White Chocolate Beverage.*

Sick of milk chocolate? Are the little ones whining for a change? Still want something silky and smooth on a cold winter's night that's chock full of calcium and vitamins? Try McFetridge's new White Chocolate Powdered Beverage. Only one hundred calories of sweet indulgence, so you can enjoy it too. But first, anything nagging at you? Anything you want to get off your chest?

The camera swept to a rolling hill to follow two approaching figures. How peaceful, how serene, how well-kept were these grounds for the dead. The two figures were identical to one another, and to me.

"Esther? Minny?"

Esther looked like she'd landed in from another stratosphere. Minny looked good though, if not a bit too thin. Clear skin, as though she'd been drinking a lot of water.

"What is this? I thought this was the Cuckoo's funeral? Why are all these people here? And cameras? And Bette?"

"Esther baby, this is Bette's show."

Esther stood back with her arms folded tight against her chest as though she didn't trust herself not to fall apart if she didn't hold herself together. The half-moons below her eyes were caverns, the edges dry river beds. I imagined her limbs falling off one by one, bone by bone, clinking to the ground like children's blocks. Her pursed lips screamed in silence *Help Me*. Did she expect me to sweep her up and quilt her back together? She was now the spitting image of a rag doll. Minny pulled a tissue from her purse and waved it like flag.

"Peace accord?"

Bette stepped in front of the camera for a close-up, and to block my sisters and me.

"So good to see all the Starlings back together again at last. What an honor to have your reunion on my show, *The Witching Watching Hour with Bette Bunting*. Welcome girls to *This is Your Afterlife*! Prepare yourselves for a walk down memory lane. You'll see just how good you had it before you even knew you had it. We have gathered here today to pay respect to not one, but all three of you! It's all your After-lives, darling Starlings! And for a final twist, we managed to find a very special person as our first surprise guest."

Two more show producers led a frail woman down the hill by either arm. She wore a pillbox hat and a dress in a not-yet-cool-again vintage style. The collar looked like a doily.

"Please clear the way for the original Mrs. Georgia Starling, that's the original Georgia Starling, the one and only Cuckoo, mother to the Starling darlings! Otherwise known as: Mom!"

ℂUCKOO

A silence can be broken with a single word that speaks to many lost years such as
Proud
or Mother
or How
or
"Where the hell have you been?" I interrupted this pastoral scene.

"It's not like she ran out for milk, Pearl," Esther said. "Yeah, where the hell have you been?"

Minny, the little wimp, stood wringing her hands behind Bette, behind the camera. Her face revealed that she hadn't been in on this twist. The Cuckoo approached us, her daughters, women now, and examined the contours of our faces with her fingers. When we were young we'd trace letters on her bare back and ask her to guess the words. I wrote "panther" every time and she never guessed correctly.

"You think I left you? I pushed you out so you could fly! And look where you landed. Far away from home, thank god. If it wasn't for me you would have been stuck in that dump, probably would have ended up at the five-and-dime, or selling souvenirs by the roadside, or working, wasting your artistry, like me, in some empty bar. Really girls, you should thank me. And look at you. All grown up. And beautiful, that always helps. Successful, yes?"

"No ma, we're no better off."

"Speak for yourself," I said. "I made it, and I'm happy. I'm a star now, Mama. But no thanks to you."

"Actually, technically, it *is* thanks to her. Without her negligence we never would have met Bette, and done all the stuff that followed." Minny, she really could be such a drag.

"Mama, Pearl dropped me." Esther the tattle-tale, pointed in my direction.

The audience gasped.

"It's true," Minny said. These two, always ganging up on me. "I was there. I watched Esther lean back and wail into that song and Pearl just let go. Her fingers released the grip like she was dropping a feather. And Esther's body weaved back and forth in slow motion, left, right, left, right, a little up, a little down, a little up again. But when she landed it was with a thud and a crack and I remembered she was a human, she was my sister just like me with a breakable body."

They all turned to me to confess. A confession is some sort of assumption of some sort of ultimate truth. An exposé of a guilt that is impossible to operate under while the years pile on top of one another. Shame and motive go hand-in-hand. But what if there are none of those things? What if one's motive is impulse and impulse is one's body because one's body is merely a muscular spasm? Who is to blame for the regrets of a life? Only you my dear, the finger on the dial points at you square in the face. You, you, you, and you. The past concludes time and seals it shut. It is only the reaction that matters for a future, that brings the unknown into focus. If you squint your eyes you can see how these reactions will shape your destiny. That horizon line? That obscured structure down the road? That's you later. To destine is the same as to doom. And I was raised to remain wily, alert, and adaptable, flexible even, to avoid doom.

Don't ask me why I did it. I'm sure you thought a lot about what you did, why you chose your wife, your career, that instant soup over an elaborate veal scallopini? I'm sure you mulled it over, chewed on it, digested it, unpacked, worked through, sent that choice through your intestines, let it fester and ferment in your bowels and then I bet you shit out the most perfectly shaped decision. I think what separates a healthy mind from a damaged one is that the healthy mind can intervene on a foul thought. Can't scratch your crotch in public, someone might see and that someone will tell someone and then every time you see someone at a cocktail party and they just slightly, just ever so slightly smirk, you'll think, gosh they know I have no manners. Every time you want to steal something, jump the fare on the subway, throw a mewing cat across the room and teach the thing a lesson, a healthy mind stops you and says, no, there is another way. And that way is to suppress this thought and move on as though you never had it in the first place. But every once in a while a healthy mind gets lazy or tired and forgets to send you these reminders. That's when a teeny-tiny eensy-weensy fissure can appear. Just wide enough so an impulse can dash through and seal the opportunity shut and bam it's too late, you've already gone and done the darn thing. You've thrown the plate, shoved the kid, smacked your wife, stolen the tips, or, like me, dropped your baby sister twenty feet from a chipboard coconut tree in front of a cheering audience. On New Year's Eve, no less. A day for fresh starts turned to an abrupt ending, a year started as an infidel, a wretch without an act anymore. Don't misunderstand, I'm not trying to excuse what I did, I'm not trying to claim insanity. I am 101% bona fide certified sane. I just may have to work a little harder than the average Jane or Joe to resist committing violent acts.

It started with sneaking salamanders to the edge of a paring knife, then the incident with Pearl the horse, the words turned against friends, and evil thoughts shot at Minny and Esther and the Cuckoo Georgia. The only time I could quell this anger was while performing. I brought my anger to the stage and twisted it into an effortless command of my own body. I was the inverted volcano, filling up with hot lava. Minny was earth, practical and driven, a bit dull. And Esther, well, Esther was pure air. She was the untouchable, the gifted. And in the laws of the universe, fire can't trump air, unless it fills it with smoke. And even in that case, air is merely masked, transformed momentarily as an illusion.

I was a kid watching my career unfold and collapse into a plateau. We'd been performing the same five acts day in and day out for months and the audiences were thinning by the week. Sometimes it's clear who is going to rise to the top when the boat is sinking and Esther was that person. We were supposed to have the same body, but we did not. She knew hers better. She could let hers float, like that cream, to the top, and I watched as everyone else took notice and angled to skim her off. Minny had her books and couldn't care less about the stage, but I, I still had that volcanic lava in me, and no one wanted to see me blow up.

You see, each time a rational mind retains focus, and the beastly thoughts recede, that seam, that original tear, remains. We never fully heal. The wound seals up but the pattern of raised flesh provides a trail of crumbs for impulse to follow whenever it feels so inclined. And here at that sensitive spot your jealousies, your hangups, your regrets, your what-have-yous, distract that healthy mind again and the escape route re-appears. This was the seam at which my temptations tore as my corporeal self went through the motions of a routine I'd done a thousand times before, dressed as a cockatiel to sing show tunes. Me and my two sisters, we tripled, we identical. So, I'm sure you can imagine life after such an event turns into a constant observation of yourself. I envy the unconscious. I am no longer sure if what happened to me happened to me at all but instead happened to Esther or Minny. Maybe I am Minny, watching Esther fall, or the other way around. Maybe I am Esther dropping Pearl and I've been watching myself tumble. Maybe it never happened at all.

Sometimes our lines abut and cross with the lines of others. And what if our fates, destinies, lucks, and choices do not lead to where we imagined? What if that obscured structure is a Shangri-La? The place is always unreal and unreachable. Or worse, what if the structure is our future selves become someone we dislike? Hate, even. To be the naif is to be the moral idealist. To ignore one's mortality is to be stuck in an identity moratorium. Might as well bury oneself right now in this dupe of a grave.

"You let go of my hand," Esther was shouting at me now. "You're not the person claiming to be the Pearl we all once knew."

Cut to the audience with hands over mouths, heads shaking in disbelief, or otherwise bowed.

"Do you remember when I took you fishing?" the Cuckoo interrupted. "Your father had returned from one of his cockamamie trips with five fishing rods. Failures from his sales, no doubt. We went to the end of our dock and sat there for hours, just waiting. I thought this is how you teach a person some patience. After a while, Minny, I believe it was you, caught a small fish no bigger than the palm of my hand. Rockfish, maybe, but what do I know? I thought we would fry it up for dinner, maybe with some cole slaw or something, but you girls insisted on keeping it as a pet. I said, *all right, let's fill a bucket with water and put your little pet in there and I'll scrounge up something else to eat.* It was hot, so I bet I made us sweet corn. I could eat three ears of sweet corn in one sitting, I loved it that much. I can't eat it now, though. My teeth can't handle it.

"We put that fish in the bucket and it flipped and flopped and you girls squealed with delight. That fish was gorgeous, I must admit. Pink and salmon and orange like exotic fruit mixed with silver metal. Each scale shimmered in a different opalescent color. I swear I saw each individual scale waving at me, like a flag swinging in the wind. This fish had rainbow eyes and long and luxurious fins. *This fish has feathers*, I told my husband, your father. *Come see*!

"He told me I was dumb, that no way did this fish, or any fish for that matter, have feathers. That I was making a 'conjecture.' *What about flying fish?* Pearl, you asked that. I felt so proud of you. Maybe the proudest I ever had. *Yeah what about flying fish?* I asked him. *All an illusion*, your father said. *Just like these fish scales, it's just light reflecting. That fish dies and he becomes plain ol' gray like the rest of 'em. He ain't gonna die.* Pearl, you said. My heart swelled. I vowed to keep that fish alive for you girls.

"Long after you went to sleep, I snuck out to check on the fish. The moon was full and lit up the entire sky. Its reflection made another tiny moon for the fish to keep in her bucket. She was swimming, less scared than earlier, slowed down. The moon turned her pinks in to blues but underneath, underneath I could see where the pink still was. The scales were still waving. That fish had turned her skin inside out. Then I saw her eyes weren't made of rainbows but diamonds. I saw that and the awe in my heart turned to greed. We could use the money. The eyes were no small thing. That's why I did what I did.

"Next day you three come barreling out of the trailer calling *here fishy, fishy* and laughing. I was there waiting, hands on my hips. *Girls, you remember the box turtle?* I asked. *Yes*, you said. *Well, remember when he got hungry and ate all the toads we caught from the pond while we ate our own lunch? Yes*, you said in unison (which never ceased to stun me, what harmony!) *Well, he did it again. Must have got her in the night.* And I showed you the bucket with no fish in it. I swear you all cried in perfect harmony too! You could do alto, tenor, soprano. I dreamed we would all sing together one day.

"That night—the night I took the fish eyes— after I did it (it wasn't so bad) I watched as each scale flipped from blue back to pink, one at a time, like a dealer flipping cards. And then, one by one, the scales fells from the body, becoming thin flint stones. Under the moonlight, the flesh was blindingly white. It glowed, girls, I tell you, it *glowed*. But it must have been too hot because the flesh also wore away to flint and only the skeleton remained. The bones were full of holes, spores, the surface the same as the moon above me and the moon in the bucket. I put those diamond eyes in my pocket and buried the fish out back with the mare. I spread the flinty scales with my foot to mix with the gravel. It was just a fish and you were young so I knew your memories of the loss would not last long. But I think of that fish not every day, but just about. I did what I had to do. But when I went to the pawn shop to sell those diamonds, all I had were fish eyes."

"Here is where I come in. I was born by a

lake to no one in particular in a house full of bunk
beds near a marsh trembling with water moccasins.
I dipped my mud-pie-sodden palms into the water
and felt three burning suns fall into my hands. They
dissolved when I resurfaced, my fists hanging tight
to keep the sensation safe, and reappeared as three
orbs.

"In one, I see I am tending a garden. It is mid-
day and I am sweating profusely under the noon sun.
I am hoeing fallow land into neat rows. The earth
looks deep and healthy and moist. Earthworms
populate the mounds and surround my boots. The
whole earth turns to slugs. Then it went to snails.
Then discarded shells. I crunch the shells into more
rows with the back of my spade. I run the result-
ing sand through my fingers and form a rock, then
a boulder. Then I roll the boulder to the edge of my
field. I repeat this process over and over again until I have surrounded my field with a fence made of
mammoth rocks. I have built myself a gorge.

"In the second orb, I am flying an airplane.
One of those old bi-planes from romantic stories of
bygone eras, stories of those explorers of deserts or
dusters of crops. Only in my dream, I am invisible.
Or rather, I perfectly match the color of the sky. I
wear celestial blue camouflage. I have complete control over the plane yet my hands are up close to my
shoulders, feeling the air wash over them. I am steering the wheel by telepathy. The plane begins to nose
dive and I tumble head first out of the cockpit, land-
ing on my feet in a jungle. My skin changes to match
my new surroundings: a deep greenish brown. I take

out a knife and carve a chunk out of a tall tree. I carve all the way through until I can stand upright in the center of the tree. I build stairs as I carve higher and higher, and when I'm about three quarters of the way up, I carve a window. I find my fallen airplane and remove the headlamps, carry them up to my tower, and shine the light up to the sky. I have built myself a lighthouse.

"In the third orb, I can't see but I can distinguish small human forms, they must be children, moving around in colors. I seem to be standing in front of some mirror, or window. I take my hand and wipe the surface clear, revealing a lake populated by families in summertime. There are picnic tables, paddle boats, slides and see-saws, children jumping off piers and flying off ropes into the murky lake. I see myself paddling around in the center of the lake. My boat gets caught in what I think are rocks but turn out to be hundreds of turtles. I circle the mass of turtles until I shepherd them into an approximation of a circle. I tie each turtle's head to head of the turtle next to them until I've made a bit of a net. I dock my boat and climb across the slowly undulating mass. I have made myself an island.

"My heart begins to beat faster, in an increasing rhythm of inhaling and exhaling. My lungs are now the size of hot air balloons and I realize my pattern of time has become out of step. I feel as though I've just flown across the world. The weight, and sound, of my beating chest, alongside my labored breath, are in equal measure. I burp one last perfect orb and see that within it, I have made myself a song.

"Across the lake I saw three women dancing and throwing strips of something into the air. String? Fabric? Paper. The strips floated to the ground and populated in mounds. No, it was packing material. I discovered a trough lined with ice and set up with wooden sticks and a bucket of caramel. I made myself a candy then licked the sugar off the trough. I saw metal spikes piercing my organs, shriveled to raisins, releasing the air in a slow leak. Eight heads rolling, one to go.

"I've never been able to understand the human eye. What we are accustomed to calling 'dark' and 'light' it sees as nuanced shapes and color. The eye is as quiet as things come. And for this, I cannot trust it. The three women were now seated on the pile of packing peanuts with their feet touching, creating a triangle between their spread legs. They held themselves up by the rods of their backs and firm stomachs, and fought against the air with chicken-bone arms. They butchered the air in a performance of jealousy and rage, frustration of *why can't we just be left alone?* They were falling and standing and bending, marshaling a god or goddess or nothing at all. This was a dance about failure. I expected them to fail. I expected they would get in the way of their own bodies and perform the labors against themselves. And they would. I knew because these three women would become my daughters.

"I started as a cocktail waitress at the Little Bad but worked my way to a spot on stage after years of enduring the backbreaking work of carting toppling beverages to smarmy men. I used to sing in the back and one day the manager took notice. Luck had it that someone had quit that very night. So, the manager offered me a supplementary job: in addition to my duties as waitress I could sing a few nights a week at the witching hour, so long as I made it worth his while by showing a little skin. I took the offer and sang songs suited to the bawdiness and the joie de vivre of the Little Bad bar. Some people accused me of hitting the bottle too hard but really I was doing it to enhance my act. I developed a sultry rasp from all the whisky and the cigarette smoke. I was looking to cash in on the hard-boiled dame trend in Hollywood, providing a little counter-balance to the wholesome small-town attitude in Sandpiper Springs.

I thought maybe I'd find my fairy tale ending here. You know the story: poor pretty girl from the sticks takes up work at a bar on the wrong side of the tracks. Girl meets hard-edged man and, at first, refuses his advances. But he's a softie at heart, and she falls fast. And, turns out, he's rich, and they spend the rest of their lives drizzled in kisses and diamonds. You might think my would-be husband was one of these men, but no, my would-be husband was the Little Bad's dishwasher.

"The dishwasher had a reputation as a fighting man with a temper and a handsome and rugged face. Temper is such a strange word, isn't it? I doubt the connection between any of its defining origins. It can mean both to restrain and measure and to tend toward outbursts. It can mean fiery or to make things proper, or to let scalded milk cool. His temper was the point at which stretching led to measuring. He pushed things to their limits and then recorded and codified the results. He was much older, with no point of origin, and nothing to his name. He'd made a small name for himself as the star of the local wrestling team, running champion in the smallest weight class at a lissome ninety-eight pounds. I found his moods charming, and he was something I could grab hold of in case it all went to pot.

'That nose is a sign of bad luck,' my superstitious aunts would say—there were six in all. I never paid them any heed, they were all holed up like cattle at the end of the world with nothing better to do than chew cud.

"Maybe it was silly, the amount of care I put into a lounge act in a desert town, but it I felt something was owed to me—the universe gave me this part as an olive branch for all the rest of the muck. On stage nights, I washed in the large basin out back behind our trailer, using a propped mirror to apply lotions, oils, and creams. I was thorough with my face powder, and had a steady line on my eyes and lashes. I only added a little color to my cheeks, as I had a naturally rosy complexion and wanted to look the part of the ashen and wanton *exotique*. Besides, after a night on stage, paired with a couple of drinks, my face changed from the color of whey into something like red clay.

"I relaxed my body and improved my skin by adding orange oil to my bathwater. Later, I'd pass these tricks on to my daughters but they were skeptical about their effectiveness. They should have listened to me, though—I bet they could have avoided all those nasty skin problems later in life. I spent good money on my costumes, too. No pinching pennies where luxury was called-for. I had a pair of long silk leopard-print gloves that I relished placing on my sylphic arms, slowly, slowly, each millimeter of the soft fabric touching my skin from my fingers to my elbow.

"I sang each night for three hours, sometimes four. I developed a brand-new way of singing the likes of which no one had ever heard. I blew the words through my two front teeth like whistles. I figured it would set me apart.

> *A wife, born poor, a farmer's girl*
> *mom and Pop hurt for cash,*
> *no bread, no milk, to fill their mouths*
> *a man driven to steal potash.*

> *A weed, green leaf, and regal herb*
> *a crone, old witch, a deal:*
> *give me your first born i'll let you be*
> *handshake, it's done, child's wail.*

> *Rapunzel ne'er saw it comin'*
> *we take what we're given*
> *thanks Pop for sentencing me*
> *to a lofted prison.*

> *For she was born, she became trapped*
> *her step mom calls: hair hair!*
> *and the obedient child obeys*

done deal, what's fair is fair.

Witch warden, has a change of heart
at night you can go out
the girl dresses to the nines
to enjoy a drinking bout.

Clever girl, changed her name and dyes
her blond hair brightly red
witness protection program, y'all
witch mom believed her dead.

A dreamer! a romantic gal,
a basic bitch for sure.
Who cares! give her a break, chrissakes
with what she had endured.

"The gambling men dropped their chips as I sang and fought for my attention after my set. I was the It girl of Sandpiper Springs. I noticed the dishwasher fought with anyone who got too greasy with me, or anyone with a philandering look, for that matter. One day a man threw a bottle of gin at me but the dishwasher had quick reflexes and he boomeranged that bottle of gin right back at the man who'd thrown it. I was stuck.

"I wanted a small wedding. The reception was at the Little Bad. I'd been staying in one of the rooms on the top floor, so this was home to me. The manager gave me away. I wore the same dress I was to wear that same night on stage: a long-sleeved and form-fitting black gown, with a sheer neckline studded with sequins at the angular shoulders. Little Bad catered the whole affair. For my wedding present, the dishwasher bought me a brand-new trailer parked on the other side of the town near the river. He wanted to get me away from the Devil, but I hesitated. This trailer wasn't the castle I was told I'd get upon betrothal. But, at least it shined.

"I haven't a clue why this man loved me. I was cruel to him. I already sold my soul willingly to the Little Bad and the Little Bad was where my soul would stay for eternity. I had to go there to keep myself alive. It was the glaring difference from the rest of my life, I think, that I craved. We made our daughters on our wedding night. I never expected to be so fertile. Carrying three bodies sucked my spirits dry. The dishwasher said I screamed so loud during the labor my singing voice left with the echoes. While he listened, my husband rolled me cigarettes and fed them to me in between contractions. The labor was excruciating and long. One, two, three (the doctor wanted to stop at the second but I told him, hold on, I'm not done yet), identical and screaming walnuts. Anyone who tells you babies are beautiful is feeding you lies. From the day of their birth, I kept a close and suspicious eye on those babies.

"The dishwasher decided he needed to make more money to support our family. He started to leave more often for a month here, and a week there, but never returned with any more cash than what he had when he left. He was always coming back with useless toys for the girls and doodads for the house. While I didn't give a damn about that albatross man,

I certainly was jealous of his freedom. And one day, he stopped coming back at all. I didn't know what to tell my girls so I told them nothing.

"I was lonely at the trailer so I swept up my three chicks and took them with me to the Little Bad. For a year we slept in the janitor's closet on a single cot. I rigged up a fence made from chicken wire to keep the girls from falling off the edge. After a year, the manager told me that the four of us were taking up too much space and forced us out. He said having kids around disturbed the customers.

I recognized an innate command in Esther, the kind that others would squelch from jealousy. Minny was the quiet calculating type. And in Pearl I saw myself, a girl grasping at desire through any means necessary. Pearl was a bitch but she was my favorite. Minny was sweet but a pushover, or worse, a worrywart. And Esther was conceited and I didn't have time to indulge her fantasies. Besides, she was one of those kids you just knew was going to be all right on her own. It was hard work keeping track of three girls, and me a young and practically single mother. Pearl would come home and stick her dirty fingers in the dinner pie first thing, before even saying hello to her dear mother. I'd catch her hand and tell her, save that for later.

"Maybe I should have just let her have a slice. Can these things explain my actions? Possibly, but probably not. Still. A mother is a human. Let that explain.

When the girls were twelve I found out the Little Bad was going under. That it was going to new owners who were going to fix it up into some high-end motel for rich folk who came to the desert for vacation or to dry out. I said, don't you think those nice folks will be needing some entertainment? They laughed and said *not the kind you would give*. They said they had no room for amateurs on their bill. When I said I didn't want to leave the only place I ever knew as home, the new owners of the Little Bad told me

"'It'll be a nice transition.'

"Said I'm

'Approaching a new chapter in my life.'

"It's true, and now I'm at the last chapter. A body in a bed with a mouth gaping wide and eyes with nothing in front of them but a popcorn ceiling and a broken lightbulb. It's funny, they call death 'going peacefully' but there is nothing peaceful about it. Who knew I would be the old woman lying face up on a single bed in a room with a nightstand and a lamp. I wonder what it'd feel like to run my tongue across the sharp peaks of that ceiling. The light intensifies and blows the bulb, leaving me in the dark. Just as my eyes are about to adjust, the sound of church bells rises.

"In the end, you all abandon me. I'll die alone. All my life, all my years, is concentrated in the tips of my toes. My life moves from my piggies to my ankles and paralyzes me in that lumpy bed. It moves up to my knees, my thighs, my you-know-what, my stomach, chest, and lingers on my lungs and takes my breath, my song, my life-blood. It pops my eyeballs out of my head (was that the breaking bulb?).

It sits on my chin and the tip of my nose, and then, poof lights out, shut down for good. Then there will be this less than a second, an eighth of a second, perhaps, where all that life oozes in my brain and tests it, like a melon for ripeness. And finally, I'll be flicked away. And that's it. There's nothing peaceful about it. All death is violent. And after death, it's all in the present tense."

Imagine three beautiful things. Anything at all. They can be a person in your life, an object from your childhood, a piece of clothing you love, or an ethereal thing, like laughter. One beautiful thing is salmon scales. Those glistening ricochets of light and opalescent color. Those objects of sacred geometry. The fatty unctuousness. Another is the smell of a stack of fresh paper, fresh from the press. The satisfying sound of running a finger across multiple folds, the fragile material snapping into place. Tssssst. A third beautiful thing is lost to the holding place of memory. A fog. A headache from trying so hard to retrieve it from those confines. Fuzz squiggles horizontally across the planes of a brain behind closed eyes in that effort. Grey, white, black striations giving way to royal blue and fuchsia with flecks of orange and yellow. A steady buzz, or tinnitus tunes to fragments of voices. An armed robbery on 24th and. Only 12.99. But we killed her seven years ago! Out of the park! The striated layers swirl into images of humans, homes, landscapes, more beautiful things. The salmon scales are lost in the din.

Now imagine the lights of a television intensify just as eyes adjust to the darkness, and the sound of church bells rise. The bells give way to phone calls and the sound of a car pulling up on gravel and an old TV turning again through stations, fuzzing, and increasing in volume.

This is your life.

ⓞNE AND A TWO AND A ONE TWO THREE

After Bette's intervention, or ambush, and after mother had been escorted away like the guest star of our lives, my sisters and I wandered in a daze to the local A&P. I picked up a red plastic basket and nodded as a sales clerk greeted us.

"Hello madams, thank you for choosing A&P. Please let me know if I can help you find what you're looking for."

We chose a chocolate sampler box to take home to Minny's bachelorette apartment. She lived in a crummy neighborhood but, hey, it was one street away from the beach, and steps from the boardwalk, so it wasn't all bad. Down we went, playing an old favorite: Russian roulette with chocolates crammed in the card stock box, choosing heart-shaped, cubed, and squared confections from fluted paper chambers. Whoever chose the cherry bomb won the game. We tuned the TV to a show about a genie. In this episode, she was sailing on a sugar cube and spilled hot water on her ship, melting her only means to land.

When do children stop tormenting one another? When do they discover this is social suicide? At what

age does a child understand she must cast the rough
ore of animal instinct into hard and human metal?
When are the snakes no longer mythological playthings, but something to fear? Now the beds were
whittled down to one, the nights were no longer a
game of outdoing, and the dreams of waking up a
diamond, came true.

The stage had welcomed us and promoted us
to prophets of comedy, song, and dance. In comedy,
laughter is in cahoots with the monsters. But melo-
drama doesn't translate to real life and at the end
there is no final swan song. Our mother needed to
lean on other people to help lead her away. There was
no arched rainbow descending from rafters and children joining hands to sing in a semi-circle. There was
no box stepping, no fireworks, no wide angle long
view panorama. There was no technicolor. In the end
we're fish flopping along, rapidly cycling through the
moments of our beautiful lives. My story is full of
boring bits but is also punctuated by joy, surprise,
pain, sorrow, and loss. That's the interesting stuff.
The worst feeling, I think, is regret. It is maddening
to wonder what if, to imagine the alternative story. It
is maddening that we cannot change the past, which
was once ours to maneuver and influence. We can go
one way or the other, or often times, we can choose
a third way. What are the consequences of missing
fate? Imagine a life where Esther didn't fall. We all
went on to great acclaim. That one show written up
in every newspaper. Stardom. Hollywood. Awards.
Bette started an all-female production house. Minny wins directorial acclaim. The world ends again in

constellations, interstellar Academy speeches.

Esther enters the small but prestigious world of dance acclaim. Kiki tours as a musician, Charlene joins the ballet, June stars in a hit and long-running comedy serial. Imagine further back. Georgia never leaving. Us girls never having to fly the coop and growing up in the trailer park, attending shock, never being nurtured as young artists. Bored with school and our own mediocrity. Young marriage and unhappy spinsterhood. Nine to fives and pattern keeping. Prodigal talents gone to waste, it's all been a game of pretend. Instead, all the chips fell where they may.

The absurdity lies in the attempt to retell any story at all the way it was first told, without missing certain details, nuances, contexts, without adding anecdotes, without using humor to soothe whatever trauma occurred. In this case, the trauma was a little wound. Perhaps only little with time and distance. At the moment of violence, the wound was the biggest thing. It became an insurmountable crevasse, a gash in which entire hearts could escape. This is an effort to stitch a story and wound back together. To find the escaped heart and stuff it back inside for another go-round. Love is a novelty, a difference, and time spent together erases those distinctions. Thus, the love goes away, or seals shut.

Esther's hands, in no hurry, chose the tranquil poison. She pointed to Minny's window, saying, "The sky's the limit." Her electric golden teeth in an ecstatic lineup reflected the glare of neon lights outside.

"I'm going out there."

"Out where?"

"You don't mean…"

"I do. I mean the sea. Sometimes you have to grab the bull by the horns, ladies."

"Or the bird by the beak?"

"I'm going to go find that bird."

"I'll help you. It can't be hard to find a parrot in the ocean. Easier to find a parrot in the ocean than a camel in a needle, or whatever that old saying is."

Esther opened the door to the balcony, crying: "Here birdie, birdie! Here birdie, birdie! Parrots mimic right? Maybe he'll respond: here birdie birdie!"

Minny followed her outside, also calling for the bird. I laughed and stood back as my two sisters wound their way down the steps from the balcony to the street. From the street they weaved through the crowd toward the beach. They ran up and down the sand before gingerly entering the ocean calling: *here birdie, birdie.*

"I'm afraid our star bird has flown too far. Parrots want nooks of trees, not endless seas!" I shouted at their backs.

"We aren't giving up! We went through a lot of work to get here," Esther shouted back.

"That bird is a breeder if I ever saw one. It could be worth a lot of money."

But birds don't work like that. I wanted a diverse aviary, well-curated, a little of this, a little of that. Esther and Minny were running up and down the beach, hooting and hollering, *hoot hoot hoot hoot!*

"Girls, maybe we're doing this bird a favor if

we let him fly!"

It was no use, I had to give in and join the search party. I threw my shoes off and ran down the steps. The sand underneath the night sky was cool and damp. I tiptoed to avoid unseen jellyfish or beached stingrays, wincing at every touch of seaweed at my feet. A thousand ships in a bottle were washed to shore. From where the water met the beach, I held my arm up at a ninety degree angle to the sky. A massive black bird with red tail feathers landed on my shoulder.

"Did you see that?! I conjured him! He chose me."

"It's a massive black bird with red tail feathers!" Esther yelled to me.

"Quick, do you have any hair ties?"

"Remarkable! Truly remarkable! You see, who was seeing things now?" Esther, always rubbing it in, always finding the sweet and sore spot.

"You see, you see!" The parrot squawked.

"Did you hear that!? He said 'you see'!"

"Parrots do have a knack for mimicry." Minny had finally caught up.

"What I meant to say was: na na na!" I told the bird.

"Na na na!" The bird told me.

"This is utterly dull. What's so great about a parrot in the sea? It would be much more interesting if it were a merman or the Loch Ness monster." I was glad to see Esther was getting her chutzpah back.

"Considering parrots are generally only found in the tropics and that this particular breed of parrot is practically extinct, I think it's fairly interesting." Minny said.

"No one believed me. There he was, I saw him, I have quite the eye. What to do with you, bird? What to do?" Esther stroked the bird's beak.

"What is the name of that director you love, Minny?"

"Jean-Paul Devereaux?"

"I bet Jean-Paul Devereux would lap up a story like this! *Rare black bird found off the south bay coast. Harbinger of luck. Good or bad? Watch this season's hottest tv show: 'seaBIRD' to find out!*"

"You're such an opportunist, Pearl. I'll phone him up now." Minny dialed on her palm and held it up with thumb and pinkie extended to her right ear. "Hey J-P, I got a swell idea. How's about a boring story about a bird?"

"Well, we can make it more interesting. Involve more birds. Maybe the three of us fall in love with the birds."

"I don't believe it…" Esther was staring through her binoculars toward the moonless sky.

"What? What is it?"

"It can't be…"

"Is it your Loch Ness?"

"Your beloved Mr. Devereaux?"

"No! It's another one of those damn birds!"

"It can't be!" I snatched Esther's hands and placed them over my eyes. She winced at my action and cowered in defeat.

"Another red-bellied?"

"I don't see anything," Minny squinted and

spun in circles.

"There! Just off the rocks, about a quarter mile in. You see?"

"You mean that red dot? That's just someone's bathing suit."

"No, no, it's definitely one of those red-bellied boobie birdies!"

"Let me see!" Minny now grabbed my hands and I let her take them from me.

"Maybe we have his friend. Hello! Hello bird! Do you two know one another?"

"You're ridiculous."

The parrot piped up: "Two know, two know!" followed by the caw of the second bird: "Two know, two know!"

"You see? They do know one another!"

"Well, I'll be damned."

I thought, things haven't been so bad. We could have had it way worse. We toured, we danced, we sang. We entertained. I've nothing more to wish for. The TV genie crossed her arms and blinked her eyes and the room went dark. The credits rolled.

❀

In the case of old televisions, screens often appeared to remain on, even after the user had pressed the cushiony "off" button many, many times. One would expect the color to go black, but the heat behind the glass emitted a mauve glow, suggesting that there was more to come, or, perhaps, we were still in commercial break. This caused much confusion for folks awaiting an ending. What's more, old televisions were known to spontaneously turn back on by their own volition. The scratch of voices rising to an audible pitch in the middle of the night snuck into the dreaming minds of American families. Double beware if you are apt to fall asleep in front of the television. The waves will secrete into the {living room, den, dining room, bedroom} and, as a wave needs a place to land, will find you, mouth agape, remote in hand. Through the mouth, up the nasal cavity, boom, into your brain. Now you're seeing in technicolor, now your mind is the episode, the director and directed.

The Starling sisters are asleep on the couch, layered on top of one another. The two big birds are pecking at crumbs on the table. The television screen blips and blurts, the mauve focuses to an image, then two, then two more, until finally, a tableau. It is an empty kitchen. Everything is boxed up and packed away. Two offscreen voices speak.

"Psst. Hey. Over here. Yah, to your left. On your left shoulder. Hey. How's it going? What's that? Yes, I am a dust bunny, good guess. Related to lint? I suppose that's true. I never thought of myself that way. Huh, I guess I am more adaptable than I thought. I can be in your belly or your dryer! Haha! What a thought. Anyway, whatcha workin' on? Can I see? Oh interesting, hm. I don't think I would have done it that way, but what do I know."

"Yeah you should probably just give up. Who am I? I'm your Sweet Tooth. What do you mean, where did I come from? I've been here forever, lady. I'm starving, can we get a snack? You know what I could make us? A chocolate cake! A devil's food cake! Super dark and moist. With chocolate frosting. Or are you more of a fruity dessert person? I could make a pie or a crumble. Peaches? Cherries? Peach and cherry?"

Lights up. We're back on Sweet Tooth's BAK-ESTRAVAGANZA! The young woman—someone new—Dust Bunny, and Sweet Tooth sit on the floor of the now-empty kitchen.

"Today we're making DEVIL'S FOOD CAKE. The cake of temptation. Get excited! This is the cake of all cakes, the piece de resistance, the creme de la creme de la crop!" Sweet Tooth is dressed like a Halloween Lucifer. Dust Bunny wears a witch hat. "First thing first, organize your ingredients. We have flour, butter, sugar, CHOCOLATE, eggs, vanilla, baking soda. Next, measure out nine cups of each and combine them all in one big mixing bowl."

"Sweet Tooth, I don't think that's how…" The new girl pipes up. She's shy, with a bland and unoffensive looking face.

"Then you mix your batter well with a wooden spoon. Where did I…" Sweet Tooth looks around, she twirls once, twice, and then is spinning like a dervish. "Hey, have either of you seen my wooden spoon?"

"Nope." Dust Bunny pretends to empty his nonexistent pockets. He comes up only with soot.

"Sorry, no."

"What in the world…." Sweet Tooth stops spinning and teeters around the room gathering her bearings. She stops and sees that the kitchen has been packed up, or begun to be packed up. The drawers and cabinets are emptied. The floor is populated by sealed cardboard boxes labeled KITCHEN in black permanent marker.

"Who packed up my kitchen?!"

"Oh, that's strange. I didn't even notice! Do we have any cereal?" The new girl says.

"Don't spoil your dessert! It'll be done in a flash. I just have to unpack these boxes and find…"

Sweet Tooth rips apart boxes and throws the contents all over the room.

"Now, Sweet Tooth, someone went through a lot of trouble packing these away. How would you feel if someone undid all your hard work?" Dust Bunny follows behind her and re-tapes the opened boxes.

"Well, that is sort of an irrelevant question, because I'm a baker and the undoing is eating and eating is the whole point of baking!" Dust Bunny and the young woman look stunned. Sweet Tooth has never ever said anything as smart as this sentiment.

"Touché. But still, I'd maybe hold off on baking today."

"Nonsense! I'll make do with what I have! People baked for millennia without wooden spoons. They used their hands!" She dives into the black batter up to her elbows and stirs with fervor. The mix splatters all over her body, Dust Bunny, and the woman.

"Fantastique!" She steps back to admire her work. "The mix is ready. Now, we butter our pan." She goes to the fridge. It too is empty.

"What the! Where is the butter? Where is my milk?"

"No milk? Guess no cereal then." The new girl looks despondent with her head buried in her hands.

"Excuse me, may I see your purse?" Sweet Tooth taps on the girl's shoulder with a single claw.

"Sure." Sweet Tooth sorts through the large tote bag, crawling inside and emerging with a trial-sized container of lotion.

"In depression-era baking, homemakers had to

make do! So, they used their hair creams as grease for pans!"

"Ew! No they did not!" The woman tries to grab her purse back but Sweet Tooth's arms grow long and she holds it up to the ceiling, keeping it out of her reach.

"Actually, Sweet Tooth is correct." Dust Bunny chimes in. "They certainly did! You see, all the cows died during the war on account of all the farmers being drafted and no one being around to take care of 'em. So no cows, no butter. No butter, no cake. And that wasn't gonna fly with those little kiddies! There was almost an elementary school revolt. The moms were at loss. What would they do to keep their little ones in line? One day Rosie the Riveter was at her wit's end trying to placate her kids with a little treat or two with no butter so she took her hair grease and swiped a pan, laid in the batter, stuck it in the oven, and there you have it. On that day there was Cake."

"Is that where shortening comes from?" The woman climbs on a stool and grabs her purse back safe and sound.

"Precisely! May we all follow in the footsteps of such an upstanding woman." Sweet Tooth holds a salute. The woman and Dust Bunny do the same.

"Ok! Now that our pan is greased, we pour in our yummy mixture and spread it evenly with our... oh right. With our... may I see your purse again?"

"Sure. I wonder who packed the kitchen up? That was rude to not ask us if we needed anything first."

"We spread it with our...with our...wallets!"

She emerges from the purse holding a gilded billet-fold.

"NO!" The woman takes her wallet and puts it under her shirt.

"We spread it with our hand! Just like the ancients did! Now we're ready to put it in the oven. Oopsie, I forgot to preheat. I always do that."

The woman begins to dance across the linoleum. She twirls the bottom of her shirt as though it were a tutu. "I'm thinking of writing an opera. I'll call it 'Lover's Aria': Vivian and Ann start from opposite sides of the misted forest. Paper maché hilltops in backlit neon undulate in the background. Pastel paper trees, collaged out of teeny tiny bits and pieces sway and flutter in the slight wind. Vivian and Ann walk toward one another, the tails of their tuxedos trailing behind them, picking up dust and leaving behind a trail of glitter."

"Oh, go on!" Dust Bunny is trying, and failing, to dance with the new girl. His tight grimy curls are beginning to fray and he can't keep himself together when he moves too much or too fast.

"Vivian and Ann are now face to face, they reach to grasp the other's hands. They just barely don't touch. We realize, then, they are blind. They stand facing one another for seven minutes or so, the length of a typical aria. Then, grasping at air, they walk past one another, and exit from opposite sides of the stage.'"

"Oh! So they were blind! Why do operas always have to be so sad?!" Dust Bunny bawls. His eyes well with water and spill out over the chocolate.

The moisture causes his entire body to sag.

"It's true! No one ever finds their love in operas!" Sweet Tooth is crying, too. A glove hands her a hankie and she wipes her tears, leaving a streak of chocolate across her cheek. "Oh well done, well done! Speaking of well done, who wants cake?"

"Did you finish baking it yet?" The girl stops dancing.

"No, but we can eat the batter! That's the best part anyway. Licking the spoon." She realizes there is no spoon and notices her covered arm and begins to lick that instead. She gets really into it and curls into a corner, transforming into a catlike creature with rock candy for teeth and claws.

"Gross."

"Darn, I was looking forward to this cake. Devil's Food is my favorite."

"Really? I always took you for more of a sponge cake kind of gal."

"Dust Bunny, that's rude."

"I don't know...you just strike me as spongy in nature."

"That is quite possibly the weirdest and rudest thing anyone has ever said to me. I think you'd be an icebox cake because you, my dear, are a cold-hearted ice princess."

"That's quite possibly the truest thing anyone has ever said to me. Yes, I'd most certainly be an icebox cake. Probably vanilla."

"Ice box cake! What a great idea for next week's episode!" Sweet Tooth purrs from the corner.

"Why does she keep talking about episodes?"

"So you like it? The opera?"

"Sure. I wouldn't read that. I'd see it though!"

"This is no fun anymore. And someone has been packing away all our stuff. I'm ready to move on."

"Move on to where?"

"Yah, move on to where?" Sweet Tooth is back at the counter now, half monster, half cat.

"I dunno, I'm just ready to move on."

"Can we move on?"

"Sure, why not?"

"How do we move on?"

"We move all at once."

"You two go ahead, I'll catch up. I'm gonna finish this batter." Sweet Tooth slinks back to her treat.

"Ok, on the count of three we go."

"Ok."

(*TOGETHER*)

"One."

"Two."

"Three."

The woman and Dust Bunny disappear, poof, leaving traces of flour behind on their seats. Sweet Tooth looks around mischievously, dips her hand in the batter up to her elbow again, retreats to her corner, and licks the length of her arm as the television fades out.

MEG WHITEFORD

Meg Whiteford is a writer, art critic, and theater maker. Her writing on visual art and performance has appeared in *Artforum, Aperture, Garage,* and *X-TRA.* She is the author of *The Shapes We Make With Our Bodies* (Plays Inverse, 2015), the Curator's Choice for the 2017 BAM Next Wave Festival Reading Room. This work was performed at the Women's Center for Creative Work (Los Angeles, 2016) and The Hive (Brooklyn, 2017). Her work has been staged at Pieter Performance Space, Steve Turner, PAM, REDCAT, Machine Project, and Coaxial. She is a 2018 Guernica Fellow and a 2015-16 REEF Residency awardee. Her latest work of theater will premiere at the 2018 PICA Time Based Art Festival. *Callbacks* is her first novel.

THE PLONSKER SERIES

Each year Lake Forest College Press / &NOW Books awards the Madeleine P. Plonsker Emerging Writers Residency Prize to a poet or fiction writer under the age of forty who has yet to publish a first book. The winning writer receives $10,000, three weeks in residency on the campus of Lake Forest College, and publication of his or her book by Lake Forest College Press / &NOW Books, with distribution by Northwestern University Press.

Past winners:

- Jessica Savitz, *Hunting Is Painting* (poetry)
- Gretchen Henderson, *Galerie de Difformité* (fiction)
- Jose Perez Beduya, *Throng* (poetry)
- Elizabeth Gentry, *Housebound* (fiction)
- Cecilia K. Corrigan, *Titanic* (poetry)
- Matthew Nye, *Pike and Bloom* (fiction)
- Christopher Rey Pérez, *gauguin's notebook* (poetry)

For more information about the Plonsker Prize and how to apply, visit lakeforest.edu/plonksker